Y
late,
Dad

You're late, Dad

Edited by
Tony Bradman

MAMMOTH

First published in Great Britain 1989
by Methuen Children's Books Ltd
Published 1991 by Mammoth
an imprint of Mandarin Paperbacks
Michelin House, 81 Fulham Road, London SW3 6RB

Mandarin is an imprint of Reed International Books Ltd

This volume © 1989 Methuen Children's Books

ISBN 0 7497 0146 3

A CIP catalogue record for this title
is available from the British Library

Printed in Great Britain
by Cox & Wyman Ltd, Reading, Berkshire

Contents

Foreword

When I was asked to put together this collection of short stories, I jumped at the chance. I thought it was a marvellous opportunity to ask some of today's best writers to produce stories on a subject that's always fascinated me, something we often take for granted and don't think about very much – the relationship between parents and children.

Of course, stories written for children have always featured parents. How could it be otherwise? Parents loom large in all our childhoods. They are the first, and probably the most important people we encounter in our lives. They are our earliest sources of love and security, and sometimes anxiety. They tell us what to do and what not to do. They influence us in many ways, some of which we hardly understand.

All this, and more, is reflected in the stories in this book. Some of them, like Brian Morse's *Flooding the Sahara* and Andrew Matthews' *Love, War and Families*, explore what it's like to live in ordinarily crazy families. Mick Gowar's *Mum's Best Boy* deals with unusual devotion for a mother, while Hazel Townson's *Scarecrows* looks at what happens when a boy tries to change his mum into the sort of parent who doesn't mind him looking a mess.

Seeing your parents in a new light is the theme of

two of the stories, Jan Mark's *Dan, Dan, the Scenery Man*, and Michelle Magorian's *The Greatest*. In the first, a child sees a side of her father she's never seen before, and learns a lesson about the way everyone acts in life. In the second, a boy realises that his father can be vulnerable, too.

In *Treasure Required*, Ann Pilling sensitively explores what happens when a delicate network of relationships between parents and friends is disrupted, while Jenny Nimmo deals with the effect of a long-hidden family secret in *Tree Talk*. And as the child of divorced parents, I wanted to include stories which reflected the experiences I remember. In my own story, *You're Late, Dad*, I've tried to show a father and a son both trying to come to terms with being members of a family that's broken up, something the heroine of Trish Cooke's *Grow Up, Maxine* is having to deal with, too.

I don't claim that the stories in this book explain everything there is to know about parents and children. The subject could never be exhausted; each new family, each new relationship between a parent and a child is unique, although you may recognise yourself or your family here and there in these pages. They don't offer solutions, either. But I hope they will make you laugh, that they will move you, and above all that they will make you *think*.

That's what stories are for, after all.

Tony Bradman   *January 1989*

The Greatest

'Boys' group,' said the teacher.

The second group of girls broke away from the centre of the dance studio, their faces flushed, their skin streaming with sweat.

A skinny girl, whose fair hair was scraped up into a bun, smiled at him, and pretended to collapse with exhaustion against the barre.

'Kevin, aren't you a boy any more?' asked the teacher.

'Oh yes,' he exclaimed. 'Sorry.'

He joined the other three boys in the class. They were waiting for him opposite the mirror.

'You've been in a dream today,' she said. 'Now I expect some nice high jumps from you boys, so we'll take it slower. That doesn't mean flat feet. I want to see those feet stretched. First position. And one and two.'

Kevin brought his arms up into first in front of him and out to the side to prepare for the jumps.

He loved the music the pianist chose for them. It made him feel as if he could leap as high and as powerfully as Mikhail Barishnikov. He knew that barre work was important but he liked the exercises in the centre of the studio best, especially when they had to leap.

But today all the spring had gone out of him. A lead weight seemed to pull him down. Bending his knees in a deep *plié* he thrust himself as high as he could into the air.

'I want to see the effort in your legs, not your faces,' remarked the teacher as he was in midspring.

They sprang in first position, their feet together, and out into second with their feet apart, then alternated from one to the other, out in, out in, sixteen times in each position, sixteen times for the change-overs.

'Don't collapse when you've finished,' said the teacher. 'Head up. Tummies in. And hold. Right everyone, back into the centre.'

It was the end of class. The girls made wide sweeping curtsies, the boys stepped to each side with the music and bowed.

'Thank you,' said the teacher.

They clapped to show their appreciation, as if they were in an adult class. Kevin knew that was what they did because in the holidays he was sometimes allowed to attend their Beginners' Classes in Ballet, even though he was only ten. He was more advanced than a beginner but at least the classes kept him fit.

Everyone ran to the corner of the studio to pick up their bags. It wasn't wise to leave any belongings in the changing rooms. Too many things had been stolen from there.

The teacher stood by the door taking money from those who paid per class, or tickets from those whose parents paid for them ten at a time, which was cheaper.

Martin was standing in front of him, pouring out a handful of loose change into the teacher's tin. His father disapproved of boys or men doing ballet so Martin did it in secret and paid for his classes and fares by doing odd jobs. His only pair of dance tights were in ribbons and his dance shoes were so small that they hurt him.

Kevin handed his ticket to the teacher.

'I saw your father earlier on,' she said. 'Whose class is he taking?'

'He's not doing a class. It's an audition.'

'Is that why your head is full of cotton wool today? Worried for him?'

'Not exactly,' he said slowly.

He tugged at Martin's damp T-shirt.

'Dad gave me extra money today. I have to wait for him. Want some orange juice?'

'Yeah,' said Martin eagerly.

'Let's grab a table.'

They ran down the corridor to the canteen area and flung their bags on to chairs.

'I'm bushed,' said Martin.

'Were you sweeping up Mr Grotowsky's shop this morning?'

'Yeah. And I cleaned cars. Dad thinks I'm

working this afternoon, too.'

'What if he checks up?'

'He won't. As long as he doesn't see me he doesn't care where I am.'

'Doesn't he wonder why you don't have any money when you go home?'

'No. I tell him I spend it on Wimpy's or fruit machines.'

Although he was only eleven Martin had already decided what he wanted to do with his life. He had it all mapped out. First he'd be a dancer, then a choreographer. His idol was a tall thin black American teacher in the Big Studio. He had performed in and choreographed shows in the West End. Professional dancers and students sweated and slaved for him, arching and stretching, moving in fast rhythms, leaping and spinning. There were black ones there too, like Martin. One day one of those black dancers would be him.

Some of the students were afraid of the teacher but they worked hard to be allowed to get into, and stay in, his classes.

'Get a classical training first,' he had told Martin abruptly when Martin had plucked up enough courage to ask his advice. So that's what Martin was doing.

'What's the audition for?' he asked.

'A musical.'

Kevin put their beakers of orange on to the table.

'So what's the problem? Don't you think he has a chance?'

Kevin shrugged.

'Which one is it?'

'*Guys and Dolls*. He's going up for an acting part. He thinks his best chance of getting work as an actor is if he gets into a musical. He says no one will look at him if they know he's a dancer. He says directors think dancers haven't any brains.'

'I'd like to see them try a class.'

'Yes. That's what Dad says.'

'Is it because you're nervous for him? Is that it?'

'No. We had a row this morning. We just ended up shouting at one another. We didn't talk to each other all the way here. Even in the changing room.'

'What was the row about?'

'About him auditioning for this job. I don't want him to get it.'

'Why? He's been going to enough voice classes.'

'Yes, I know,' he mumbled.

For the last year his father had been doing voice exercises every morning, taking singing lessons, working on scenes from plays at the Actors' Centre, practising audition speeches and songs, and reading plays.

'I didn't think he'd have to go away, though. This theatre's a repertory theatre and it's miles away. I'd only see him at the weekend. And even then it'd probably only be Sundays. And if he got it he'd start rehearsing two weeks after I start school.'

'So? You've been there before. Not like me. I

start at the Comprehensive in a week's time. It'll be back to Saturday classes only.' He swallowed the last dregs of his orange juice.

'Want another? Dad said it was OK.'

'Yeah. I'll go and get them.'

Kevin handed him the money and pulled on his tracksuit top over his T-shirt even though he was still boiling from the class.

He couldn't imagine his father being an actor. But his father had explained that he couldn't be a dancer all his life, that choreographers would eventually turn him down for younger dancers and, in fact, had already done so a couple of times. He had to decide which direction he wanted to go in before that started to become a habit.

For the last two years, since Kevin's mother had died, his father had only accepted work in cabaret in London, or bit parts in films, or had given dance classes. Otherwise he had been on the dole. Kevin was used to him being around now.

When his mother was alive and his parents were touring with a dance company, Kevin used to stay with a friend of the family. Dad said it would be like old times staying with her again. Kevin didn't want it to be like old times. He wanted things to stay just as they were.

He pulled on his tracksuit trousers, dumped his holdall on his chair and waved to Martin.

'I'll be back in a minute,' he yelled.

He ran down the two flights of stairs which led to the entrance hall, past two of the studios there and downstairs to the basement where the changing rooms and other studios were.

Outside the studio where the audition was taking place stood a crowd of people peering in at the windows. They were blocking the corridor so that dancers going to and from the changing room had to keep pushing their way through with an urgent 'Excuse me!'

The door to the studio opened and six disappointed men came out. Kevin's father wasn't among them.

Kevin squeezed in between two people by one of the windows and peered in.

Inside the steamed-up studio a group of men of every age, height and shape were listening to a woman director. A man was sitting at a piano.

The director was smiling and waving her arms about.

'Here. Squeeze in here,' said a dancer in a red leotard. 'You can see better. They're auditioning for *Guys and Dolls*. It's the men's turn today.'

Kevin didn't let on that he knew.

'She's really putting them through it,' said the dancer. 'First they have to sing on their own and the MD, that's the man at the piano, decides who's going to stay. Then they have to learn a song together.'

'What's the song?' asked Kevin.

' "Luck Be a Lady Tonight." Know it?'

Kevin nodded.

Know it? As soon as his father had heard he had

been given the audition every song from *Guys and Dolls* had been played from breakfast to bedtime.

'Then they have to do an improvisation. The director chooses who to keep out of that lot and then the choreographer teaches them a dance routine.'

The dancing would be kid's stuff for his father, thought Kevin. He wiped the glass. His father was standing listening. So, he'd passed two singing tests. Now it was the acting.

The director was obviously explaining what the scene was about. She was pointing to individual men.

'She's telling them about the characters,' said the dancer.

Kevin felt angry. How could his father go through with it when he knew that Kevin didn't want him to go away? He observed his father's face, watched him grip his arms in front of himself and then quickly drop them and let out a breath.

'Excuse me!' he said fiercely, and he pushed himself out of the crowd and along the corridor to the stairs. And then he stopped. He remembered the look on his father's face and realised it was one of anxiety. It astounded him. He had seen his father upset before, but never scared. Why would he be scared? He was a brilliant dancer. But now, of course, he also needed to be a good actor. He was trying something new in front of actors who had been doing it for years and some of those actors were younger than him. That took guts, as Martin would say.

Kevin hadn't given a thought to how nervous his father might have been feeling. He knew how badly he missed the theatre. To start a new career when you were as old as him must be hard; harder too when he knew that Kevin hoped he would fail.

He turned and ran back down the corridor, ducked his head and pushed his way back into the crowd to where the dancer in the red leotard was standing. He wasn't too late. They hadn't started the improvisation yet. He stared through the glass willing his father to look at him.

The director stopped talking. The men began to move, their heads down in concentration as she backed away.

Please look this way, thought Kevin.

And then he did. He frowned and gazed sadly at him.

Kevin raised his thumb and mouthed, 'Good luck!'

At that his father's face burst into a smile.

'Thanks,' he mouthed back and he winked.

Kevin gave a wave and backed away through the crowd and along the corridor.

It was going to be all right, he thought. If his father did get the acting job he knew he'd be taken backstage and he'd meet lots of new people, and at least he wouldn't be touring so he could stay with him sometimes. And Martin could come too. And Dad would be happy again.

Martin wasn't at the table. Their bags were still there with the two plastic beakers of orange juice.

Kevin knew where to find him. He walked to the corridor. Martin was gazing with admiration through one of the windows into the Big Studio. His idol was giving a class to the professional dancers.

He grinned when he saw Kevin.

'Guess what!' he squeaked. 'I was by the door when he went in and he noticed me. And he spoke to me. He looked at my shoes and he said I ought to swap them for bigger ones at Lost Property and then, you know what he said? He said, "Say I sent you!"'

He turned back to watching the class and sighed.

'Isn't he the greatest?'

'Yes,' agreed Kevin, and he thought of his father. 'Yes, he's the greatest.'

Hazel Townson

Scarecrows

'Honestly, you look more like a scarecrow every day,' Mrs Ormrod complained to her son Mervin. 'Why can't you smarten yourself up a bit? You don't see Brian Bosworth walking about like that.'

Mervin scowled his bionic scowl, which would one day turn his mum to pigeon-spattered stone. But not yet; Mervin was biding his time.

Mrs Ormrod wrenched Mervin's tie from one side of his neck to the other. Mervin gagged, pretending to be throttled.

'And that's enough of that! If you're trying to wangle a sick note out of me you can think again. You've had more time off this term than a broken clock.'

Just then the doorbell rang, and there was Brian Bosworth, standing to attention on the doorstep, smart as a guardsman. Brian grinned a clean, sparkling grin which Mrs Ormrod matched with a tender smile.

'Oh, come on in, Brian love! Our Mervin's nearly ready. He's just got to brush his shoes and comb his hair and clean one or two nasty marks off his anorak. I was just telling him how smart you always look. I never see any nasty marks on *you*.'

Brian flicked shiftily at an invisible speck on his

19

neat lapel while Mervin drove lasers of hate into the back of his mother's neck.

At last Mervin was ready – or at least his mother couldn't keep him any longer without making him late for school. So she pushed her son roughly out of the door, saying, 'Oh, go on with you! You'll have to do! But I don't know how Brian can shame to walk along with a scarecrow like you.'

Round the first corner, Brian said: 'Your mum does go on a bit, doesn't she?'

'Yeah, well, it's your fault,' grumbled Mervin, who was jealous of Brian for not even *having* a mum. 'Why d'you have to look so tidy all the time? Can't you muss yourself up a bit before you ring our bell?'

'It's my dad,' Brian explained. 'He's worse than your mum. Won't let me set foot outside the door unless I'm what he calls "properly turned out". You don't think I enjoy it, do you? I'd rather look like a scarecrow any day.'

Suddenly Mervin stopped walking.

'Let's show 'em, then!' he muttered vindictively.

'Show 'em what?'

'Show 'em who's boss, of course. If we want to look like scarecrows then we will. And what's more, we'll make 'em like the idea. We'll even make 'em beg for it.'

'Oh, yeah?'

'Yeah! I just got this new book out of the library all about Transference of Ideas. It claims you can make anybody believe anything. We could make

20

our folks believe it's good to look a mess. It's all a question of ancient Eastern powers of mind-over-matter, mixed up with modern Western technology. "Transfers ideas with astonishing power," it says. I guess you could put any idea into someone's head and keep it there, so that, short of dying, they'd never get rid of it. You can make 'em believe their legs don't work, and stuff like that.'

'You don't say?' grinned Brian disbelievingly.

'Just wait and see; you'll be amazed. I know *I* was when I read some of the experiments that succeeded. We'd need to borrow your dad's computer, though. You start with a picture of the person you want to transfer your idea to. You tape that to the back of the computer. Then you type your message in, together with loads of details about the person you want to pass the message on to. Then you have to relax completely, close your eyes, place the palms of your hands on the computer screen and concentrate hard. There are some extra words you have to type in as well – a sort of formula – only I'll have to look those up in the book; I've just forgotten what they are.'

'Sounds daft to me,' mumbled Brian, though by now he sounded more alarmed than scornful.

'That's what they told Columbus when he said the world was round.'

'Anyway, I'm not supposed to touch my dad's computer. He'd kill me if he caught me.'

'He's not going to catch you. You're not telling me he never goes out of the house, even if he does work from home? We just bide our time until he's away for a nice, long stretch.'

'No!' cried Brian forcefully. 'If anything went wrong with that computer my life wouldn't be worth a bag of crisps.'

Mervin shrugged.

'Well, if you'd rather be miserable for the rest of your school days . . .'

He began to walk away.

Brian hesitated, pondered, frowned, then slowly began to follow in Mervin's wake.

They spent the rest of the month practising relaxation – Chapter 2 of the Manual – and became so good at it that one night, when Mrs Ormrod took cocoa up to Mervin's room, she found them both fast asleep on the floor.

'Here, I thought you two were supposed to be doing your homework? And fancy lying about on the floor in your good school uniforms! I never heard the like!'

Next they started compiling dossiers of their parents' statistics; birth dates, height, colour of hair and eyes, identifying features, likes and dislikes, all that sort of stuff. This involved some subtle questioning and not a little snooping, but at last the deed was done.

Stealing the photographs was easy.

('Can I get the family album out? We're doing this project on the 1960s and we're supposed to take pictures to school to show the fashions and that.')

As for working out the wording of the idea they wanted to transfer, that was no more difficult than any English composition. By the middle of October they were ready to move into action. All they needed was the computer.

The trouble was, Mr Bosworth seemed glued to the wretched thing. He was engaged in a rush job, working a ten-hour day, including weekends, and at the end of each session he was too tired to do anything else but throw a meal together and then crawl off to bed.

'We've got to get him out of the house,' said Mervin. 'If we don't get a move on, these dossiers are going to be out of date, not to mention us having nervous breakdowns.'

'I could pretend to be ill,' suggested Brian. 'He'd have to go with me to the doctor's.'

'Charming! You go off with him and leave me to do all the dirty work.'

'Well, it was your idea.'

'You've chickened out, Bosworth!'

'No, I haven't! I'm helping you, aren't I? Risking my dad's computer and all. I'm just not as keen as you are, that's all.'

'Right!' said Mervin grimly. He had already made up his mind to miss Brian's dad out of the experiment altogether, and serve Brian right. 'How can you tell how long you'll be in the doctor's surgery?'

'It's never less than an hour. And if by some fluke we're quicker than that, I can pretend to feel sick at the last minute and dash outside. Then I'll lose my turn in the queue.'

'Well, that's not the only snag. Suppose your dad can tell you're not really ill?'

'Back trouble,' explained Brian confidently. 'Nobody can ever prove whether you've really got back trouble or not. Did you know that ninety per cent of the world's population have back trouble at some time in their lives?'

There seemed no alternative; Mervin would have to go it alone. They chose the sixth of November which was a Tuesday and part of the half-term holiday. This being the day after Bonfire Night, Brian could pretend he had strained his back cavorting round the bonfire on the waste land near the house. The boys had already 'borrowed' the spare front door key, and Mervin had worked out a direct route to the computer, which was upstairs in the spare bedroom Mr Bosworth called his study.

'Ooooh, my back!' Brian woke up moaning and groaning, pretended to need help getting dressed and actually refused his breakfast.

'Right! Back into bed!' ordered Mr Bosworth. 'I'll send for the doctor.'

Brian was horrified.

'Oh – er – well, it's not quite that bad. I think I can stagger round to the surgery.'

'Maybe. But I don't fancy sitting in there half the morning. I've got work to do.'

'They've speeded up the queue a lot lately.

24

Mervin said he was out in ten minutes the other day. And you shouldn't call the doctor out unless it's really urgent. There are posters telling you that all over the surgery. If you waste the doctor's time he might not be able to visit somebody who's really dying. Just think, Dad, if you had that on your conscience for the rest of your life . . .'

It was touch and go, but Brian managed it in the end. Almost exactly to plan, he and his father set out for the surgery and Mervin sneaked in.

Soon after lunch, by which time Brian's affliction – particularly his appetite – seemed to have responded well to the doctor's prescription, Brian was just about to ring up Mervin for a quick gloat over the success of their plan when Mervin's mother rang *him*. Mrs Ormrod's voice did not convey her usual approval of Brian's righteousness.

'Now then, Brian, you just send our Mervin back home for his lunch right away. He's already half an hour late.'

'But – he's not here, Mrs Ormrod.'

'Not there? Well, he said he was going to your house.'

'Well – er – I've had to go to the doctor's this morning, so I expect he found I wasn't in and went somewhere else.'

'Such as where? He's nowhere round here, and it's not like him to be late for his food.'

'Try the playing fields,' said Brian without

conviction. Somehow he felt vaguely uncomfortable. Where on earth could Mervin be?

Two hours later, Mrs Ormrod rang again. This time she sounded very upset indeed.

'Now, look here, Brian. I've wasted I don't know how long searching round for our Mervin, and now Mrs Ellis tells me she distinctly saw him unlocking your front door at half-past nine this morning. I don't know what you two think you're playing at, but I want that lad back here right away.'

'But I told you, Mrs Ormrod, I haven't seen him.'

'Come on, now, Brian Bosworth, I'm not as daft as you two think I am. Either our Mervin's at your house or he's disappeared off the face of the earth. And another thing, whose is this nasty old scarecrow you've dumped in our front garden?'

Grow Up, Maxine

I put on my Walkman that Dad had bought me for Christmas. I didn't want to listen to 'them' any more. I put the volume up really loud so I couldn't hear them. They could hear me, though. The ching-ching sound grated on Mum's face. It was more interesting watching her reaction than listening to her whining voice.

'Let's make a day of it, nah? Wha' you say? Eh? Let's make a day of it?'

She scowled and tried to make it look like she was not interested in my sulk. My big brother Roy was still biting his nails. He slid the comic he had been sitting on on to his knee. He did this carefully so they would not notice. But I noticed and I thought it was rude. I wanted to be rude. I stamped my feet and clicked my fingers. Closed my eyes tight. Made the words with my mouth letting no sound out.

'Baby baby baby . . . ah oooh . . . yeah yeah yeah . . .'

Mum lit another cigarette.

'Come nah, Maxi? We'll make a day of it,' she pleaded again, pulling the cord from the tape machine and leaving the lead dangling from the earphones on to my lap. She really wanted to go to the zoo.

'I don't want to make a day of it,' I protested. 'When Dad comes I want to be here.'

The boyfriend touched Mum's elbow. He thought I hadn't seen, but I had. I sighed loudly and made my way upstairs.

Roy followed.

'Mum wants you,' he muttered. I ignored him and threw myself on my bed. He was just the same as them. Traitor. Ganging up on me. He'd start making me feel guilty soon, saying I should go and apologise. Get my coat and sit tight in the back of the boyfriend's car. Go to the zoo. Play happy families. But I wasn't going to. Not this time. It was *my* birthday. And I wanted to wait for *my* dad. He'd promised.

Roy sat on the floor, his back pressed against the wall. His knees up against his chin. His Nike trainers pointing in opposite directions.

'Suppose you're not talking to me again,' he teased. I put my earphones back on, but I wanted to talk really.

'Yes, I'm talking to you,' I shouted up to the light bulb. 'It's them. They know Dad's coming but they still keep going on about going to the zoo and . . .'

The phone rang and I knew. Roy did too. We

still held our breath.

'Daniel,' Mum's voice scolded, 'why you have to promise the child if you know you cannot come. It's her birthday!'

Me and Roy looked at each other and he came to sit on the edge of my bed.

'Dad doesn't mean to let you down,' he said. I started to count the daisies on my wallpaper. 'He told me so. It's just that he doesn't have time like he used to.'

'He has time for Blonde Lily,' I said, remembering the fat blonde woman smelling of Lily of the Valley perfume and stale cigarettes. We'd met her one Sunday when Dad brought us to the pub. 'He has time to take *her* out, I bet.'

'Pauline is Dad's girlfriend,' Roy defended. 'Mum and Dad are divorced.'

'Separated,' I corrected.

'They want to make new lives for themselves,' Roy persisted.

'And what about me?'

'Oh, grow up, Maxine,' he said, slamming the door as he left. The breeze knocked down the best of my birthday cards.

'Eleven Today, Eleven Today, Eleven Today,' they teased.

Mum was upset but she tried not to show it. Poured custard on the apple crumble like there was no tomorrow. She put the bowl in front of me and smiled. Roy and the boyfriend had gone to the pub and she was in one of her immature moods.

'Clap hands for Mammy 'til Daddy come, bring cake and sugar plum to give Maxi some,' she sang. 'Remember that one, Maxi?' I did. She used to sing it to me when I was about four. But I wasn't in the mood for remembering so I shrugged my shoulders.

'You really miss that bighead of a father of yours?' she provoked. I wasn't going to answer her but I wanted her to know.

'Yeah, but you don't care. You've got a boy-friend now,' I muttered. She took the apple crumble, and for an instant I thought she was going to pour it over my head. I flinched. Instead she scraped it out of the bowl and on to the plate of leftovers. I hadn't eaten any of it, but it didn't matter.

'What you miss?' she jabbed. 'You miss the noise? Eh? You miss the headache?'

I had almost forgotten the rows Mum and Dad had had before he left, but I didn't miss them. Didn't miss them at all and I didn't want to be reminded. Not of those times or the times before. I just wanted to sort out *now*.

'You have a boyfriend. You don't care for me and Roy any more. You don't care. You have a boyfriend now! You have a boyfriend . . .'

The dam had burst. I felt my cheek sting and my brother came between us. Dad was standing in the doorway with Blonde Lily and Mum's boyfriend was shrugging his shoulders and steering them in. I wanted to run to Dad, but he didn't have any arms left for me. One was holding his cashmere coat and the other was clenched firmly around Blonde Lily's waist.

'Hi,' I said, surprising myself.

'Baby,' he said, unleashing one arm, but it wasn't the arm I wanted any more. I took the coat away instead and Roy shook his hand.

'I jus' passing, yer know,' he said, taking out his wallet. His hands were shaking and he wouldn't look me in the eye.

'You wasn't going to come,' I managed to muster.

'Not true,' he lied. 'I was going to pass later. Your mother and me, baby, we not like we used to be . . .'

He took out a crisp twenty pound note and handed it to me. I decided to take it.

'I know you and Mum have problems,' I said. 'I'm not a baby . . .' I caught Roy's eye and I could see he wanted to laugh. But I went on. 'You and Mum aren't happy together, but we're not happy without you.'

The boyfriend and Blonde Lily looked uncomfortable.

Mum looked at me like she'd never seen me before. She kissed her teeth, but I went on.

'I know you and Dad don't . . .' I searched for the word, 'love each other any more, but you love us, don't you?'

For once they listened to me.

31

'Well, you've been behaving strangely. You've both changed. Trying to hide things from us. Treating us like we don't know what's going on. But we do. And when *you* get separated it shouldn't mean that we have to.' I stopped. Thought back on my behaviour for that whole day.

'I'm sorry,' I said to everybody in the room, but I didn't raise my eyes from my feet until a friendly pair of Nikes touched my toes. My brother was the best. Even if the rest were involved in their warpath I'd always have him. I took his hand and left. Dad tried to hold me as I passed, but I wouldn't let him. I just giggled and held on tight to my brother.

'We raised two good ones, there,' I heard Dad announce. I closed the door before I could hear Mum's reaction, but I guessed she'd pick up on the words, 'We raised? We? We?'

We, me and my brother, sat on the stairs and laughed.

Brian Morse

Flooding the Sahara

This summer we went on a fortnight's canal trip from Stroud, over the Cotswolds, to Oxford. Boring, I can hear you saying; what I did in my hols, by Jane Herrington, Cradley Heath, West Midlands, England, the World, the Solar System, the Universe. Yawn, yawn. The kind of story the teacher gives the first day back at school (and on paper, not in your books, because she knows you're not going to make any effort). And then canals – yuck! – smelly places full of thrown-away prams, and ducks nipping each other and making hideous noises that never sound anything like quack. Ultimately boring, you're already asleep.

Well, I thought I knew all about canals, too. But they can be quite exciting, especially when you've got a dad like mine with a bit of get-up-and-go – or should that be get-up-and-go-wrong?

To put you in the picture (Miss says you should always fully introduce your characters and not spring them on the reader, and actually I *am* writing this for her, even though I know she'll sling it straight in the bin – in fact I'm writing it for her *because* she'll sling it in the bin), here's a thumbnail sketch of my family. My dad Donald is very tall. He's not much of a swimmer, but he likes anything to do with water – which is why we finished up on a canal holiday. He has five tanks of tropical fish in the house and two goldfish ponds in the garden. Mum's very quiet, not a bad idea as Dad talks incessantly. He's got a way of thinking aloud that's very noisy. My name's Jane and my brother's called David. He's older than me (fourteen at the latest count). He's always breaking his leg playing football. So far he's done it four times. All I can think to say about that is, if football's so dangerous I'd get a note to let me off games!

The first week of our holiday went okay. It rained a bit. It shone a bit. Dad rushed about a lot, opening lock gates and paddles (the things that let the water through from one lock to another), and knocking in gigantic pins to moor the boat to. Mum made mugs of tea and cooked meals. Nothing much really *happened* except when David sat on the cabin roof facing the wrong way round and didn't notice a low bridge approaching at five miles an hour. The bridge concussed him and one or two other things, but nothing serious by David's standards. He had to spend a night in Stroud Cottage Hospital. When he was discharged in the morning (much to the relief of the nurses),

Dad fetched him back by taxi and lost his way among all the tracks through the fields. After that, at the first sight of anything over the canal, even a plane, Dad confined him to the cabin and forbade him to so much as set a foot outside.

A couple of days into the second week we were having our evening meal in a pub near our moorings when Dad suddenly got very animated and started waving the diary of our trip. David and I had been supposed to fill the diary in (to keep us good, I think the idea was), but somehow David had finished up doing it.

'I've just realised. At the rate we're going we won't get to Oxford till Monday!' he shouted. 'We still haven't got on to the top of the Cotswolds. We're supposed to be there by Friday.'

'We'll make up time tomorrow,' Mum said, reasonably.

'Even if we set off at half-past four in the morning and sail till dusk for the next four days we'll still be late!' Dad said. He'd done a calculation on a piece of paper which he started waving too.

'It's a nice clear evening,' Mum said after a bit of thought. 'The moon's out. I know it's against canal regulations, but why not travel through the night? No one will ever know.'

Everyone was surprised at Mum suggesting something so 'naughty', but David and Dad rather fancied steering the boat down the moonlit canal, with the stars twinkling, and the otters and water voles slipping in and out of the water, bats swooping down over them and owls hooting in the woods. The idea rather appealed to me, too. Within a couple of minutes we were out of the pub and piling back on the boat. We started off up the canal in search of our lost time. Who'd have thought Dad was about to flood the Sahara!

To get to the top of the Cotswolds you need to go through a dozen locks very close together. It's called the Tucker Ladder. From the bottom the locks do look exactly like an enormous staircase.

'Bags I steer first!' David said. So he did. He always bags everything first.

The moon was out. Dad stood in the bows and shouted out instructions like, 'Hard to port!' and, 'A fraction to starboard!' He was in a really good mood. Mum and I went to bed in our bunks. All was peaceful except for the sound of Dad's voice. The stars twinkled. The bats twittered and radared after the insects. The odd otter slipped in and out of the canal in case any fish were daft enough to still be up. In the woods mice scurried about with an eye over their shoulders for the owls.

'Mind the crocodile, David!' Dad called softly in the darkness. 'Have you noticed that anaconda?' Ground mist rolled in across the fields. So peaceful, so quiet, so magical – at least for a bit.

I was woken by a jolt. At first I thought it was David testing how strong the bank was, as he quite often did. I wandered on deck in my nightie. Dad was leaning over the front, using the bargepole as a dipstick.

'Not a lot of water in here tonight, Jane,' he grumbled. 'There ought to be someone to complain to.'

With a lot of grunting he pushed us off the mudbank we'd stuck on. David re-started the engine. I stayed on deck to count stars. It was just before midnight. A couple of bends and we reached the bottom of Tucker's Ladder.

'Fifth longest series of locks in the whole of Great Britain,' Dad said. 'Not many other people gone up it by night, I bet!' I nodded off for a second, but was woken by another jolt. We were in the bottom lock.

'We're hardly floating. Where's all the water gone?' David called to Dad.

'It'll be all right when we've pinched the water from the next lock,' Dad said. He ran and opened the paddles from the lock above. Water began pouring through, but not a lot happened to the water level. It rose a little, but not enough to float us.

Mum came yawning on deck.

'Put the radio on, will you?' Dad said. 'A bit of cheerful music's what we need to while away the small hours.'

Mum put the radio on. A saccharine-voiced D.J. was introducing late-night music. An owl hooted. A water vole peered from its nest on the water line, wondering where the water was.

Mum said, 'Looks like someone pulled the plug.'

'I'm going to have to investigate,' Dad said. 'Don't drive off without me!' He clambered on to the tow-path. Five minutes later he was back. 'The water's quite low in the other locks, too,' he said, 'but nowhere near as bad as down here. I've had an idea. If we open a couple more gates enough water should come down for us to float into the next lock. Then if we close that one quickly enough we should have solved our problem. True?'

'Probably,' Mum said.

David stayed behind to steer. Dad went to the one-after-next lock gate, Mum and I to the one above that. We opened the paddles. Water began to rush down towards the stranded boat.

'It's floating!' came David's triumphant shout. 'Aargh!'

We rushed back down. The boat was banging itself against the gate we'd just come through. Round it a little flotilla of ducks was floating, all protesting at being woken, at the same time asking for bread because they could see humans.

'Quick!' Dad shouted. 'Steer it into the next lock, David!' However the water was heading for a spot at the end of the lock. With an immense *Glug!* most of it disappeared.

'I told you there was a plug hole,' Mum said, yawning. 'Didn't I?'

We all peered, and there in the moonlight, we could see a hole in the bottom of the lock, quite a large one.

It might have been best to have gone for help at

this point – or just to have waited for morning – or to have gone back into the main canal and pretended we'd never gone anywhere near the Ladder, but Dad was too full of energy to leave it at that.

'I've got it!' he said. 'The water from the locks we've opened doesn't give us time to get the boat into the next lock – right? But if we open *all* the locks –'

'All the locks!' Mum said. 'Shouldn't we wait for the canal plumber?' But Dad was already on his way.

'Come on!' he shouted.

Very soon we were merrily opening all the paddles, starting from the top. 'Great idea, wasn't it?' Dad said.

It was. Then it wasn't. At first it was okay, but soon water began slopping over the tops of the lock gates lower down. Before we knew it the gates began trying to open themselves – which is the exact opposite of the way it's supposed to be. The creaking, groaning, tearing sounds they made were horrendous. And water began to arrive at the bottom lock at a tremendous pace.

'Quick! David!' Dad bellowed down the ladder. 'Now's your chance!' But by now a tidal wave was smashing the boat against the lower lock gate. 'Hang on!' Dad shouted, but with a *Thwack!* the bottom lock gate burst open and the barge went whizzing back the way we'd come from, towards Stroud. It travelled about a quarter of a mile with Mum and Dad and me running as fast as we could along the towpath beside it. Then suddenly it braked to a halt. There was a churning sound and it began to head back at an immense speed in the Oxford direction – uphill, as it were.

'Turn the engine off, David!' Dad shouted.

'Something's sucking it!' David shouted. 'Help! I want to get off of here!' He jumped for the bank. Mum just about caught him.

The boat gathered speed. We ran alongside shouting at it to stop. It entered the bottom lock and disappeared with a tremendous sort of reverse plopping sound down the hole which had got a lot larger since we'd last looked at it. 'My cassettes!' I cried. 'My pop posters!' The hole was so large it began to swallow all the water from the canal back in the Stroud direction, and the water kept coming and coming. The whole canal began to disappear.

It was a bit of a disaster, but not one you'd have called catastrophic, except Dad had another bright idea.

'We can't just leave our boat lying down there,' he said. 'The owners won't appreciate it. Let's try and float it out.'

Mum said something about wouldn't a crane be a better idea, but Dad said, 'Now, think about it. Be logical. The water in canals must come from somewhere. It stands to reason. And I've a shrewd idea where from.'

'Where are you going, Donald?' Mum shouted after him. You could tell she thought he was being hasty by the way she said 'Donald' – she usually calls him Don.

'Back to the top, of course!' Dad shouted.

Dad was right, of course. Now it was empty you could see the canal was filled from a pipe that ran into the top lock.

'Huh!' David said. 'A lot of use that titchy pipe'll be. I've seen baths fill quicker.'

'You give up too easily,' Dad said. 'Now listen! You hear that whirring sound?' We listened. 'It's a pump! And what for! To pump water up here to let it back down again! I should have thought of it before. And I know exactly what to do!'

'That's called breaking and entering!' Mum said when he told us what.

Maybe it was, but Dad said the canal people would be grateful to us for saving them a job, and in the end Mum picked the pumping station lock. Dad found the right valve and turned it full on. A torrent flowed down towards the boat.

The water came down the Ladder so fast it pushed the boat further down the hole, smashing it as it went. It might still have been okay if Dad could have stopped the water coming. When he saw what was happening he sprinted back up the Ladder to the pumping station. Unfortunately the valve had stuck.

'Oh well,' he said. 'You win some, you lose some. At least we're safe.'

Then we started hearing things on the radio (Mum had put it down on the tow-path – it was the only thing we'd got left). The first thing was a news flash for the people down in Stroud, a flood warning.

The tidal wave that headed down the canal caused over three million pounds worth of damage, though of course we didn't know that at the time. Half an hour later, the radio said the water supplies for the whole of Oxfordshire had mysteriously dried up. It was like someone had sucked the whole place dry.

'Do you think that might have anything to do with us?' Dad suddenly wondered.

'All from not being able to turn a silly tap off, Donald?' Mum said. She was using 'Donald' a lot.

'But maybe it is,' Dad said excitedly. 'Everything's connected underground. It's got to be. Oxfordshire's higher up than Gloucestershire. We've run all the water from one county into the other! Wow! To think we did that!'

'You did,' Mum said. 'I told you not to meddle.'

'It was your idea we made the journey by night,' Dad said.

'True,' Mum said.

Next day water was popping up all over the country where it shouldn't have. And then kept drying up where it should have been wet. What Dad had done by accident had set off what's called a chain reaction. The Fens ran out of water. So did the Thames – there were mudflats outside the Houses of Parliament. You probably remember them having to close the Underground because of flooding.

A week later the effects had spread all over Europe. They took a month to reach Africa. But in the end they did. And Dad had flooded the Sahara.

When Gran phoned last week to say she was coming to stay we asked her about her holiday in Majorca. 'Very nice,' she said. She was really brown. But for some reason the sea had kept a long way out. It had been so far out she hadn't got any paddling in. She'd complained to the travel company but they'd said it wasn't their fault. 'I'd really like to get my hands on whoever's fault it was,' she said.

Dad clapped a hand to his forehead when she'd rung off.

'Now just keep quiet about *you know what* while Gran's here,' he said. 'I just couldn't stand being ticked off by her. And no one outside this little group of people knows that we started all this, do they?'

'We?' we said. 'Us?'

We kept quiet though. We were sympathetic.

The trouble is, I've just got to tell someone, even if the someone's only a piece of paper that's going to be thrown in the bin.

Oh no! Miss is looking at me suspiciously. She knows I usually don't write this much. So I'll finish now. But I know she won't read it. It'll be in the bin by tonight. Won't it?

Jenny Nimmo

Tree
Talk

One day, when Will was coming home from
school, the avenue where he lived became a forest.
Huge and ancient trees loomed across his path,
blotting out the sun – then they were gone; and
Will found himself in the middle of the road with
cars hooting on either side of him.

Feeling foolish and frightened he ran on across
the road, and didn't stop until he was home.

'I had a dream, Mum,' he told Ellen, his mother.
'A daytime dream, in the middle of the road. I
dreamt that there were trees all round me, huge
and very old. Why did that happen? Am I ill?'

His mother did not immediately reply but
looked past him in a startled way, as at a ghost.
And then she said, 'Of course you're not ill. You're
such a dreamer. You've probably been reading
about forests, but you mustn't carry stories out
into the street with you; it's dangerous!'

Will was not satisfied. He sensed that the true
explanation was different. He did not argue, however, because Ellen was a secretive person who did
not like discussing strange or painful subjects.

'I see,' he said and went up to his room. But something followed him. He felt it. Unseen and unheard it had crept out of his imagined forest and come home with him.

Over the next few days Will became certain that someone else was living with them. He could hear rustling in dark corners, like footsteps in dead leaves. He could hear trees whining when there was no wind. Sometimes he found himself running in unusual places: through the kitchen; out of the bathroom, trying to escape from something that was bent on reaching him. He began to think that he was very slightly mad, and he was sure that his family knew what was happening but wouldn't talk to him about it.

And then, one evening, he received a message. It seemed to come from the tree outside his window; just a few words here and there, snatches of a conversation mixed up with pictures; a man whistling, the sound sailing round Will's head then dwindling, as though a breeze had carried it away. Something in the message sent Will racing into his sister's room without knocking.

Sarah, all in black, was sitting at her dressing-table, painting her nails with crimson varnish.

Will approached and stared at his sister's pow-dered face, at the green-fringed eyes and crimson lips. Sarah spread her ringed fingers across her cheek. 'Approve?' she asked Will's reflection.

Will did not approve. His sister looked too old, too dramatic, but he decided to keep his opinions to himself. 'Brilliant,' he said. 'Where are you going?'

'Just out!' Sarah smiled and looked sixteen again. 'Silas always finds somewhere wonderful!'

Silas Simpson was studying Russian at the Tech. He was tall and blond and drove his parents' red Volvo. When Sarah was not preparing for a forthcoming adventure with Silas, she was dwelling on their last one.

'I've had a message,' Will told his sister.

'Oh?' Sarah breathed on her witchy nails then flapped her hands in the air to dry the varnish.

'Yes,' Will went on. 'From the tree outside my window.'

'What did it say?'

'That's the trouble. I don't know. It was like getting a letter, when you know the handwriting but you can't remember whose it is, and it's in code so you can't understand it.'

'Tree talk, I suppose,' his sister said. Did she know something? Why did she suddenly look wary?

'Sort of,' Will replied.

Sarah's fluttering fingers reminded him of wounded birds and he turned his attention to the jars and bottles reflected in her mirror. He tried to read the reversed names. 'MAERC,' he muttered. 'That's CREAM, and LIO is OIL, but what's EGAS? I don't get it.'

'Sage,' Sarah said. 'It's a herb; they stuff things with it!'

It was an unusual shade of green, soft and with a hint of silver, like the delicate tracery of fungi that crept across damp branches. Will picked up the tiny bottle and retreated with it.

'Hey, where're you taking my stuff?' Sarah looked up.

'Can I borrow it?'

'It's nail varnish, Will!'

'Please?'

Sarah laughed. 'Go on,' she said. 'But don't decorate the walls.'

Clutching his prize Will went back to his own room.

Sophie, his stepsister who was six, called to him from the bottom of the stairs, 'Tea-time, and you're to come now or . . .'

Will slammed his door. He sat on his bed, unscrewed the cap of the little silver-green bottle and out came the brush. Carefully, he drew the brush across the rim of the bottle until it stopped dripping, and then he began to paint his nails. He wasn't content until three coats had been applied. This took longer than he had bargained for and he had to sit tight through Sophie's second shout, and one from Ellen. By the time Max, his stepfather, had added an angry, 'Get down here or else . . .' Will was ready.

'What the hell have you. . .?'

'Why didn't you. . .?'

Max and Ellen had a habit of leaving questions unfinished when they were angry.

'Sorry!' Will took his place beside Max.

'I told him, I did!' Sophie mumbled through cake.

'We know,' Max said irritably. He was always harder on Sophie, who was his own child.

A car hooted from the street and in answer to the signal, Sarah drifted through the kitchen on her way to join Silas on yet another mystery trip.

Ellen lifted her eyebrows and murmured, 'All in black again!'

But Max just said, 'Be back before midnight, sweetheart!'

Sarah sang something like, 'Of course,' and fluttered out.

Ellen sighed, lowered her gaze – and saw Will's right hand. 'Why are your nails grey?' she inquired.

'Sage,' Will corrected her.

'And shiny,' Sophie added.

'Well?' Ellen waited.

'We were rehearsing,' Will said, suddenly inspired. 'For the play. I'm a ghost.'

'Oh?'

'You'd better get it off before school tomorrow,' Max said, not angry now but trying to be Will's friend again.

'OK.' Will grinned reassuringly. 'I promise.'

After tea his mother made sure he kept his word and followed him to his room. Will dabbed sadly at his silvery nails. He was aware of the tree's watchful presence, its disapproval.

'I'm not giving in; I'll do something better next time, see if I don't,' he quietly told the tree.

'Who are you talking to?' Ellen asked.

'The tree,' Will said.

'The tree? Oh, I see!' She was not impatient with him this time but Will sensed a tiny tremor of alarm in his mother's voice.

Later, when Ellen and Max had shut themselves in the living room with the television news, Will made another journey to Sarah's room. This time he knew precisely what he wanted.

Next morning as he jogged to school a small flat pot tapped his chest in a comforting way from the inside pocket of his jacket. Warm spring air swirled over the grass verges and a kind of buoyancy carried him along, high and fast. Perhaps it is true happiness, Will thought, and he was aware that there had been a small fault in his smooth life, in the place that his sisters filled with tall young men or ballet classes. He wondered how things would have been if his own father had not died. So many times of late he had begun to question Ellen about his father but she always scurried away from anything that might lead to a discussion about death. 'I've told you, Fred was ill,' she'd fling at him before she rushed out to the washing-line or the coal-shed or put the hoover on, and that would be that.

In the school cloakroom he turned his back on the other boys, opened the little pot and dipped his finger in the greasy green eye-shadow. It spread across his eyelids in a deliciously oozy way, and he continued the colour round and under his eyes.

Will's best friend, Bob Haines, who took most things in his stride, was shocked when he saw Will. 'You're not going into class like that, are you?' he asked.

'Why not?' Will said.

'You look like an alien, a female one!'

Will shrugged. It wasn't bravado that sent him smiling into class. He was propelled by the minty fresh smell that bounced on sunbeams through the open windows.

And he sat there, bewilderingly happy, until Mrs Shilton sent him back to the cloakroom to remove the 'warpaint'. The children giggled behind him like a field of geese, but it didn't worry him in the least, and after school he dipped his finger into the eye-shadow again, and extended the colour from his eyes right round his face and across his upper lip, so that he arrived home with a shiny green beard.

Ellen sent him straight up to the bathroom.

'Sorry, Mum,' he called. 'We've been rehearsing again. It was so late I didn't have time to wash.'

'I hope the streets aren't full of green-faced children from Chirk Road Primary!' his mother said.

Was she suspicious? 'No, just me,' he reassured her.

The tree was waiting for him. It gave a gentle nod in his direction and he sat close to his window so that he might catch words of approval and further instruction. For he was not sure what he should do next. He thought about the tree, about every tree he had known, in every season and every colour. He thought about the strange patterns that swirled from root to branch, the scars they bore and how they cried in the wind, and into the pictures came a small thread of fear.

'Remember?' asked the tree.

'Remember what?' Will asked shakily.

But the tree just sighed and kept repeating itself.

That night Will drew back the curtains before he went to sleep and when the moon sailed round to glare into his window, he woke up to see black silhouettes of branches stretched across his window, so close they threatened to burst in on him. But instead it was the messages that came into his room. Leafy whisperings drifted round his bed and the whistling man began to talk. 'Stay there, Will. Don't move, Will.'

The sound of a chain-saw screeched across his head and the tree whined, 'Remember?'

Will sat up, his heart pounding, sweat oozing into his palms. 'Remember what?' he cried.

The moon disappeared, the tree was swallowed in darkness and couldn't answer him.

In the morning Will daubed his face like a warrior. It worried him now, that he didn't know why he was compelled to do this, but his forefinger was sure and steady as it dipped into the little pot and swirled colour over his forehead, his nose and chin.

Sophie screamed when she saw him and Sarah moaned, 'Oh, Will, not my eye-shadow!' His mother spilled tea on the cloth and Max said, 'Really, you could wait until you get to school.'

'Just wanted to save time,' Will grinned. 'It takes me ages to get into my ghost suit.' He had never found lying easy but now false explanations tripped off his tongue.

'I can't let you get on the bus like that,' Ellen said. 'Please, Will . . .'

'OK,' he cheerfully agreed and went up to the bathroom.

At school, once the rosy scrubbed look had faded, Will's face was left with an unhealthy green tinge and his eyes were ringed with dark shadows.

'I hope you're not coming down with something, dear.' Mrs Glee, the kindest of the dinner ladies, peered at Will over the chips.

'No, thank you,' Will said. He couldn't think of a better answer because he suspected he *was* coming down with something, though it wasn't the sort of something that could be treated with pills or a day in bed. Had his father suffered from this same strange illness? What had happened to Fred that was so terrible it could not be mentioned?

Mrs Shilton allowed him to fetch a drink of water from the cloakroom during the last lesson, and on his way back he raided the art cupboard and concealed two drums of green powder paint under his sweater. It was Friday. He could spend

52

the whole weekend being green.

'Will, I want to talk to you!' His mother met him in the hall, her face tense and anxious. 'I met Bob's mother today. There is no end of term play, she says. No dressing-up! No ghost costume! Can you explain?'

Could he explain? There was a tree outside his window; a tree with cool insistent fingers, tapping out messages, whistling through his sleep. He couldn't explain.

'Please, Will, no more lies. No more green faces!'

'Not even at the weekend?' he asked meekly.

'I don't think so. We're all a bit fed up with it.' She looked very smart, his mother. All ready for an evening out with Max, Will thought.

'OK,' he said and went upstairs.

The tree looked in at him with sympathy. Will wished that it was beside him, in his room, so that he could touch it and be rewarded, perhaps, with a rough hug. His mother only hugged Sophie these days and Max, of course. Perhaps she thought him the wrong age now and should do without that kind of thing until he started 'dating'. No doubt Sarah got hugs from Silas Simpson.

But I can bring trees in here, Will suddenly thought. He emptied both drums of powder paint into a tin that he'd been saving for his rock collection, ran to the bathroom and filled his tooth-mug with water. Carefully he measured the water into the tin of paint, then he stirred the mixture with his biggest paintbrush until it was a thick, drippy cream.

He began behind the bed; no hanging back; he used huge bold strokes, sweeping up and up until he could reach no further. He put a chair on his pillow and continued upwards. He piled books on the chair, climbed higher and continued the branches to the top of the wall. He moved the chair, added more books, climbed up again and swept his brush over the ceiling. Green branches now overhung his bed. Leaves danced round the light socket and glistening emerald dew dripped on to the duvet.

When the paint finally ran out Will remembered the unfinished can of moss-green gloss they'd used for the gate, and he ran down to the garage.

'What are you doing, Will?' Sophie asked, meeting him on the stairs.

To be furtive would be fatal. 'Measuring,' Will lied efficiently. 'Project for school!'

'Did Dad say you could! In your room?'

'Course!' Will heaved the two-litre can and Max's new wide brush past Sophie's threatening stare. He was trembling with excitement.

An hour later his room was a radiant forest. When he half closed his eyes the painted trees that encircled him seemed to stir gently in the spring weather while the real tree, that had begun it all, sparkled with pleasure.

Perched high on the chest of drawers, Will spoke to the tree. 'There,' he said. 'I'm getting closer; I haven't remembered all of it, but I will soon.' He flourished his brush in one last corner, stepped back, and fell to the floor.

The room swam, tiny stars, bright as frost, fluttered through the forest and Will closed his eyes.

'Will! Will! Will! What have you done?' Sophie was in the doorway looking frightened.

There were footsteps running up the stairs behind her, and Max burst into the room, closely followed by Ellen.

Max swore, rushed to Will and gently felt his limbs. Nothing was broken and with Max's help Will stood up. He smiled, sheepishly, trying to pretend he had not seen the can of spilt paint.

But his mother did not shout at him. She was standing very still, staring at Will's trees, horrified, but more than that, frightened at the sight of something that seemed to astonish rather than anger her. Was it a forest then that she had tried to banish, deliberately kept hidden even from herself? 'Will!' It was alarming how softly she spoke. 'What possessed you?' And then she ran out and a door slammed somewhere.

'You've made a terrible mess!' Max tried to sound stern and soothing at the same time. 'I suggest you do something about it! Put the covers in the bath and scrub them; the carpet will need turps, I'll give you a hand. What a stupid thing to

Jenny Nimmo

do. You've really upset your mother!'

'I know,' Will said. 'I'm sorry.'

'Why did you do it?'

'I had to,' Will sighed. 'It's too difficult to explain. I can leave the trees, can't I?'

'It's your room,' Max said. 'You'll have to live in this mess for a few years now.'

'Forest,' murmured Will.

Max went to fetch the turps, Sophie ran to tell Sarah who was reading in the garden. Will pulled off his duvet cover and took it to the bathroom. He half filled the bath, laid the cover in the water and watched green streams swirl out of the cloth. He knew he should be worried, ashamed, but all he could feel was a sort of exhilaration. He knew he'd brought things to a head.

The bathroom was next to his parents' bedroom. Will could hear Max trying to comfort Ellen before fetching the turps. But it seemed that she would not be comforted, her voice had an hysterical note. Will longed to know what they were saying. He had to know. He slipped off his shoes and socks, stepped into the bath and pressed his ear to the wall.

'It's not possible,' Ellen sobbed. 'I did everything I could to make sure he never knew. When he asked questions I always gave him the story we agreed on. He *can't* remember!'

'But, darling, why? It was a traumatic event!'

'I won't believe it. It's something else, trouble at school or, or . . . oh, Max, I don't know . . . there

56

are so many years. He was so small!'

'Darling, he's remembering, or trying to. Can't you see, all this painting himself green, he's trying to find the way back!'

Back where? Remembering what? Was he a changeling then, a forest goblin? Was his true father an ogre dressed in green? I'm stuck in that forest, Will thought, and I can't find my way out because I don't know where I began.

Max must have begun to comfort Ellen in other ways for their conversation ended and Will was left with his mystery.

His mother had, more or less, recovered by tea-time, but Will knew he was under observation; she watched his face, turned to him instantly when he spoke. She was waiting, almost fearfully, for him to find out who he was. He stared at her, through narrowed eyes, willing her to tell him. But she couldn't even talk to him.

That evening an early darkness came drifting up from the west. The trees shuddered restlessly and thunder rattled in the distance.

When Silas Simpson swept Sarah away in his red car, hailstones were leaping round the house, smacking the windows like tiny explosions; and then they stopped and a long black quietness settled over the town.

Will couldn't sleep. He lay fighting for memories, wondering at the absence of real anger about the paint, listening for messages. The storm returned. Rain clamoured in the streets and the

wind screeched across the rooftops. Will's tree
called him, insistently; he went to the window and
drew back the curtains. It was so black outside, he
could only hear the branches groaning out their
riddles. Then a raggedy moon crept out and glittered through the tossing leaves, splashing Will's
painted trees with pale, uncertain light. The storm
was invading his room.

He ran back to bed and watched his looming
indoor forest tremble and complain. The thunder
intensified, crashed overhead and Will's trees
began to move. They were closing in on him.
Gigantic arms snatched at him. Closer and Closer.
He couldn't breathe.

A deafening scream came from his tree, it
seemed to tear him inside out and in a voice, from
long ago, Will cried, 'Dad! Dad! Daddy! Dad!' to
someone who wasn't Max.

Then peace washed over him, smooth as a
stream. He smelt trees, gazed up and up at their
forever soaring trunks; they reached and seemed
to clasp the clouds, through a pattern of leaves that
spun and sang and filled his life, and he remembered.

'Are you all right, Will?' Max called.

'Yes,' Will said, truthfully. 'I was just surprised.'

'The wind has torn a branch off the sycamore,'
Max said in a retreating voice. 'Still, we can't do
anything about it now.' A door closed.

'Poor tree!' Will closed his eyes and fell happily
asleep.

He was up very early. Face washed, nails clean, not a hint of green anywhere. Ready for a new day, a beginning.

He was glad to find Max and Ellen alone in the kitchen while the rest of the house was sleeping off the night's disturbance.

'Hello!' he cheerfully greeted his parents.

'You look bright,' Ellen remarked, 'considering.'

'I am. I've remembered, you see.'

'Remembered?' Ellen looked apprehensive. She had lost the long battle for secrets, after all.

'Yes, I remember a man whistling and talking to me. He's wearing a dark jacket with orange patches on it, and a helmet so I can't quite see his face. It's my father, isn't it?'

Ellen didn't reply. Her pretty face suddenly looked crumpled. Max took her hand. It was as if they had to present a united front to face, not only Will, but someone who was stronger than both of them.

'I want to know about him,' Will persisted. 'Something happened in a forest somewhere. I was there, I saw it, but I can't put it all together properly. Please help me!'

'We're all so happy,' Ellen said evasively. 'Max is a good father, he's given you everything!'

'Yes, yes.' He wished his mother would make it easier for him. 'But knowing about my true father isn't going to spoil all that!'

'You don't need to know about the past, Will.'

She ran a hand nervously across her forehead. 'It's over. It doesn't matter!'

'It does matter,' Will cried relentlessly. 'He wants me to know. Don't you understand?' And then he found words that surprised even him. 'He's trying to say goodbye!'

Silence gripped them, took their breath, held every tiny piece of kitchen frozen until Max said gently, 'I think you'd better tell Will everything!'

And Will felt the room give a curious sigh of relief as it gathered them closer together, and Ellen speaking in a new fearless kind of voice said, 'I'll need a strong cup of tea.'

While Max filled three cups Ellen put her arm round Will. The past wasn't between them any more. She began to tell him about her days with his father. About the husband who spent his life in the forest, clearing the dead wood, caring for the trees, tidying broken branches, healing. 'Even on a Sunday he'd want to spend time with his trees,' Ellen said, a little resentfully. 'We lived near the forest then, and he'd go and talk to them. He'd take you sometimes. He was closer to you than anyone.'

'I know,' said Will, happily filling another gap in his memory.

'But I was always a little apprehensive,' Ellen went on. 'Even before the storm; he was such a carefree sort of man.'

Will knew about that other storm. It had been aching at the back of his mind for a long time; half-remembered sounds of thunder and his father's green kingdom groaning in the distance.

'It came one Friday night,' Ellen told him. She seemed glad to find that, after all, the story wasn't so impossible to tell. 'Next morning Sarah had a dancing class, but Fred *must* go to his trees. "Let me take Will," he said. So I drove you both to the forest and then went back to town with Sarah. But it was Saturday. The traffic was dreadful and we were too late, of course!'

'And in the forest?' Will asked sadly, for he knew that whatever it was that had happened in the forest that day had changed their lives, yet his mother still remembered a missed dancing class. In hiding the forest from him, she had almost managed to forget it herself.

Ellen approached the last part of her story quietly, but did not falter. 'He'd taken his chain-saw in case of surgery, in case he had to amputate a wounded branch. He found one, of course, and climbed the tree, but he was careless, he didn't notice other broken branches, the vibration of his saw set them off, one knocked him to the ground!' And then, suddenly furious again, even after seven years, she railed, 'How could he? You were only two years old. You could have been killed!'

'But I wasn't,' Will reminded her. He could see the great branch sway; he heard an ear-splitting crack as it fell towards him, and his own baby voice crying, 'Dad! Dad! Daddy! Dad!'

There had been no reply.

61

'When I came back I found you sitting on a mass of broken leaves and branches. You were sobbing and talking nonsense, to the trees, I thought. And then I saw Fred buried under the branch beside you. You were holding his hand.'

'I'm glad,' Will said, and when she looked uncertainly at him added, 'glad that I was holding his hand.'

He thought he could hear something retreating, very softly, through the house, and then the wounded sycamore spoke, or perhaps complained a little to a passing ghost as it creakily adjusted itself to a new shape.

'Sarah must remember,' Will said, suddenly resenting the way that Sarah had kept secrets to herself.

'She promised never to remind you,' Max said, defending Sarah as always. 'We thought it was for the best, Will!'

'I see.' Will hated them for that; making his own sister one of them. She could have told him the truth, might even have wanted to. 'Can we go to that forest one day?' he asked.

'Well . . .' Ellen looked at Max.

'If you think you need to,' Max said.

Will burst out, 'Of course I do! I've got to make up for lost time. Don't you understand?'

'We understand,' Max said.

Will got up and went to the back door. He was about to step into the garden when a little flame of anger caused him to swing round and suddenly exclaim, 'You should have told me all this before. Keeping it secret made me afraid it was a horror story. I'd like to have known about my dad. I could have thought about him, told my friends. People need to know their past.'

They gazed at him sadly, not knowing what to say.

'And now I'm going to have a look at that tree,' he said and left them.

The severed branch lay across the lawn surrounded by a mist of scattered twigs. Will stepped over the debris and touched the living tree. Where the storm had torn the branch away a painfully jagged stump remained; he couldn't reach it, even standing on tiptoe. They would need a ladder. He knew exactly what to do.

'Don't worry, Dad,' he murmured. 'I'll fix it!'

'Will?' His mother was standing on the kitchen steps. 'Are you all right?' She looked lost and anxious. Will was glad he'd made her sad.

'I'm fine,' he said, 'but we've got to do something about the tree. D'you think Max would help me?'

She ran towards him, her slippers flapping on fragments of leaves and shattered leaves. 'Of course he will,' she cried, hugging him. 'He always wants to help you!'

All at once Will forgave her. He saw his future stretching out before him, running in a bright path through the trees.

Love, War and Families

When Alice Warren got home from school, the rest of her family was in. Alice saw that Dad's car was parked outside the house and as she walked up the garden path, she heard Robert (her elder brother) playing his electric guitar. Robert only knew one chord, but he played it very well, fast sometimes and slow at others. Joan (Alice's younger sister) was in the front room. She was using the remote control unit to flick from one TV station to another while she listened to her personal stereo and read a book.

Alice walked through the house to the kitchen, where Mum and Dad were chopping vegetables. Dad looked up, saw Alice and said, 'No.'

'What?' gasped Alice.

'Whatever it is, the answer is no,' said Dad.

'But I haven't said anything!'

'You don't have to say anything,' said Dad. 'I can see the pound signs in your eyes!'

Alice slumped against the kitchen door frame

and picked at a scratch in the paintwork.

'It's not fair!' she sulked. 'You don't even know what I was going to say!'

Her parents worked on silently, trying to ignore her. Upstairs, Robert adjusted the volume control on his guitar until it sounded like a killer whale eating a steamroller.

'I only wanted to change my name by deed poll!' grumbled Alice.

This time it was Mum who looked up. She was in the middle of chopping an onion and tears were streaming down her cheeks.

'Change your name?' she sniffed. 'Whatever for?'

'It's boring!' pouted Alice. 'I don't like it! It's just not me! I don't look like an Alice. My friends agree with me!'

'Which friends?' Mum asked suspiciously.

'Sharon and Tracey.'

'I thought you were off Sharon and Tracey,' said Dad, doing strange things with a garlic crusher. 'I thought you were never going to speak to them again in your life. What happened to . . . who were those two girls who came round last Saturday afternoon?'

'Kim and Dawn,' said Alice. 'I'm never going to speak to *them* again in my life!'

Dad looked as though he were going to ask something, then he shook his head and did even stranger things with the garlic crusher.

Mum wiped tears from her eyes and said, 'Well,

if you and your friends don't think you look like an Alice, who do you think you look like?'

'Rayleen!' Alice replied.

'Rayleen?' sniggered Dad. 'Isn't that stuff you put in the washing machine to make the clothes softer?'

'Rayleen Holly Warren!' insisted Alice, blushing.

'What *do* Alices look like, then?' frowned Dad.

'Alices,' said Alice scornfully, 'have curly red hair and glasses!'

Mum and Dad exchanged frowning looks.

'But Alice,' said Mum, 'you *do* have curly red hair and glasses.'

'I know!' shrieked Alice. 'And I hate it!' And she burst into tears.

Robert appeared in the kitchen. He glanced at his tearful sister, shrugged and picked his way round his parents. He took a packet of chocolate biscuits out of a cupboard and began to eat them, mournfully, two at a time.

'Hello, Robert,' said Dad.

Robert glanced at his father and shrugged.

'Hello, Mum! Hello, Dad! How are you?' said Dad. 'We're fine, thanks, Robert.'

Robert pushed two more biscuits into his miserable, spotty face.

Alice fell to her knees in the kitchen doorway, sobbing violently.

'Any thoughts on your future now the exams are over?' Dad asked Robert. 'Sixth Form College?

66

Further Education? Finding a job?'

A light gleamed in Robert's eyes. He chewed frantically, swallowed his mouthful with a loud gulp and said, 'Thought I might nip down town tomorrow. Get my ears pierced.'

'Your ears are already pierced,' said Dad.

'Yeah, on the *bottom*!' Robert pointed out.

'Well, that's your immediate future taken care of! Any longer-term plans?'

Robert's face turned thoughtful.

'I'm thinking about becoming a vegetarian.'

'Does it pay well?' asked Dad sarcastically.

Robert shrugged.

'Do stop crying, love,' Mum said to Alice. 'You'll get yourself into a state.'

'I know you hate me,' grizzled Alice, 'but why do you want to hurt me all the time?'

Behind her, in the dining room, Joan twitched in a joint-snapping dance. She thrust her head into the kitchen and bawled above the row in her headphones, 'Mum-erinoo! Pop-a-ding-dong! What's for scoff?'

'Tuna fish spaghetti,' said Mum.

'Sicky slime poos!' shouted Joan.

'With green salad.'

'Super-mega gross!' yelled Joan. 'I want something else-a-boo!'

'Like what?' asked Mum wearily.

'Pasta creepies with baked-a-bim-bam-beans!'

Dad stared at Joan wide-eyed. 'Rob,' he muttered, 'she is making it up, isn't she?'

'What?'

'There's no such thing as pasta creepies, is there?' said Dad, sounding worried.

'Yeah!' said Robert. 'It's this pasta stuff, shaped like tarantulas and snakes, in a spicy sweet 'n' sour sauce.'

'Good grief!' croaked Dad.

'Mega delish-a-lim-lam!' screeched Joan.

'When, oh when,' whimpered Alice, 'will I be allowed to live my own life?'

'I don't think,' said Mum, rubbing her hand across her forehead, 'that I can stand much more of this!'

Dinner was not a great success. Robert crouched low over his plate and swept food into his mouth with arm movements like a swimming turtle. Joan used a fork to prong one baked bean at a time as she jiggled to the music from her cassette-player. Alice sat motionless behind her untouched plate and looked as though she were suffering, except when Dad poured Mum a second glass of white wine, when her expression became narrow-eyed and vicious.

'Are you secret alcoholics?' she hissed.

'Sorry to disappoint you,' said Dad, 'but no, we're not. We'd like to be, but we just can't afford it.'

'You can afford wine!' snapped Alice. 'You buy Joan loads of cassettes! You bought Robert that guitar and amplifier, but you won't pay for me to have my name changed! I'm only the middle child, so I don't count! It's not fair!'

'We do pay for your dance classes, love,' said Mum gently. 'And your riding lessons.'

'Dawn Southeby's parents bought her her own horse!' Alice countered. 'And they pay for her to see a private psychoanalyst!'

'I fancy a drop of wine, actually, Dad,' said Robert, looking hopeful.

'No chance, Rob,' said Dad.

Robert threw down his knife and fork in disgust.

'Gary Milton in my form goes in the pub with his dad!' he protested.

'Beany, beany, beany, wipe-out!' chanted Joan.

'Right!' barked Dad. He leaned over the table and switched off Joan's cassette-player. 'Listen carefully, all of you. I've got something important to say!' He waited until all his children's scowls were turned in his direction. 'The summer holidays are starting at the end of the week. Your mother and I have decided that we're going to Crete this year.'

'Big deal!' scoffed Robert.

'Smelly!' squealed Joan.

Alice said nothing.

'But we've got a surprise for you,' Dad went on. 'You're not coming with us.'

Robert, Alice and Joan all let their mouths fall open at the same time and said, 'Uh?'

'You're staying here,' said Dad. 'What we need

69

is a break from each other, or rather, your mother and I feel we need a break from you lot. So, we're off to Crete for a fortnight next Sunday.'

'But what's going to happen to us!' burst out Alice, tragically. 'You can't just desert us! We're your own flesh and blood! It's illegal to leave us on our own!'

'I didn't say you were going to be left on your own,' smiled Dad. 'It's your mother and I who are going to be left on our own – peacefully and blissfully on our own! You're going to have somebody to take care of you!'

'Who?' chorusd the Warren children.

'Your granny!' said Dad.

'Great!' grinned Robert. 'Granny Warren lets us do as we like!'

'She'll call me Rayleen if I ask her!' said Alice petulantly.

'Gran-a-boonie!' rasped Joan.

Dad's smile widened a little.

'No,' he said, 'not Granny Warren. Granny Crump!'

His smile widened a little more as his children's faces fell.

As soon as Robert saw his parents were engrossed in the wild-life documentary, he shot Alice a meaningful glance. Alice nodded and touched Joan's arm. Joan looked up from her 'Wordsearch' book, saw Robert and Alice's expressions and nodded. The Warren children gathered in the dining room.

They all sighed. Their pooled depression made the lights look dim.

'Granny Crump!' groaned Robert. 'That's really, really bad news!'

'She hates me!' whined Alice. 'I just know she hates me!'

'Mega-yukky bogies!' growled Joan.

Granny Crump, their mum's mother, lived in Yorkshire. She had a voice like a fog-horn, a face like a rusty gasworks and didn't hold – so she said – with modern ways of bringing up children.

'D'you remember those Christmas presents she sent us last year?' asked Robert. 'She sent me a spanner!'

'I got a pair of knitting needles!' sighed Alice.

'I got a thermal vest!' exclaimed Joan. The memory of it was so shocking that she spoke in English.

'She came to stay once, when I was little,' said Robert glumly. 'She took me shopping with her. She sang a hymn on the bus. Everybody was staring . . .'

'Remember when we went up to see her last summer?' wailed Alice. 'That walk over the moors! I thought I was dying!'

'Argh!' cried Joan, springing to her feet. 'I've just thought of something super-gross-horrible-mega-disgusting!'

'What?'

'WE'LL HAVE TO EAT HER COOKING!' howled Joan.

Granny Crump roasted potatoes until the out-
sides were rock-hard and the insides were empty.
She boiled cabbage until the water was green and
the cabbage was the colour of the bottom of a
pond. Her roast beef tasted like tissue paper and
she served everything up with yellow-and-brown
slabs of what she insisted was 'Yorkshire pudding'.
Her gravy had thick, floury lumps in it. ('That's
the goodness comin' out!' said Granny Crump.)
Her afters were completely awful and always
drowned in custard. Her custards had thick, rub-
bery skins that she chopped up and deposited on
the children's plates. ('I know 'ow kiddies love
skin!' said Granny Crump.)

'No!' moaned Robert. 'I can't stand it!'

'I'm going down to the station,' said Alice
unsteadily, 'and when the next train to London
comes, I'm going to throw myself under it!'

'I reckon we should zap up to Yorkshire and do
Granny in!' snarled Joan.

'She'd only come back and haunt us!' said
Robert. 'But we must do something! Two weeks of
Radio Four and bed by seven-thirty's gonna drive
me straight round the twist!'

'And *Songs of Praise*!' shuddered Alice. 'Don't
forget *Songs of Praise*!'

'There's only one thing for it!' proclaimed Joan.
'There's only one way to make Mum and Dad
change their minds about not taking us on holiday
with them!'

'You don't mean. . .?' said Robert, paling.

'I do!' replied Joan.

'You can't mean. . .?' quailed Alice.

'Yes!' said Joan firmly. 'We have to! It's the only thing that could possibly work.'

When Mum went into the kitchen to make a cup of tea, she found Alice drying the washing-up, polishing glasses with the tea-towel until they sparkled.

'There's no need to do that, love!' Mum said.

'Oh,' said Alice airily, 'I just thought I'd make myself useful for a change.'

Mum smiled to herself curiously and filled the kettle.

'Mum,' said Alice, 'Alice was Great-grandma Warren's name, wasn't it?'

'Yes, it was.'

'She's the beautiful lady in that old photo album, isn't she?'

'That's right,' said Mum, lifting the tin of tea bags down from the cupboard.

'Do you think I might grow up to be beautiful?'

Mum looked all melty and put her hands on Alice's shoulders. 'You're already beautiful, love!' she said.

Meanwhile, in the front room, Robert slumped down beside Dad's chair and looked casually at the television.

'That's that actress you fancy, isn't it, Dad?' he asked.

'Hmm!' said Dad.

'I'll tell Mum!' Robert warned. Dad laughed.

'I've been thinking,' said Robert, 'I'm gonna take a stroll over to school tomorrow and have a chat with Mr Jenkins.'

'He's the Technology teacher, isn't he?'

'Yeah!' said Robert. 'I want to find out a bit more about computers, only I don't think A levels are the best thing for me. I think Mr Jenkins will be able to tell me what other courses are available.'

Dad reached out and punched Robert's shoulder gently. 'Good for you, son!' he said.

Just then, Joan entered the front room. She was wearing her blue pyjamas and clutching a battered teddy bear. She clambered carefully into her father's lap and snuggled into him, smelling of toothpaste and soap.

'What's this?' Dad asked quietly. 'Ready for bed?'

'Uh-huh!' said Joan.

'No rows? No tantrums? No screaming hab-dabs?'

'I'm sleepy,' said Joan.

'Have you kissed Mum good night?'

'Uh-huh!' said Joan. 'Dad, please will you read me a story before I go to sleep?'

Much later, the Warren kids held a conference in Joan's room.

'How did it go?' asked Robert.

'Brill!' replied Joan. 'Dad wiggled my nose and said I was his best girl. He hasn't done that for ages!'

'Mum told me about the brace she had to wear on her teeth when she was my age again,' said Alice. 'She always does that when she's feeling sympathetic.'

'And Dad called me "son"!' said Robert.

Joan whistled quietly, well impressed.

'OK,' said Robert, 'Phase One has worked a treat! Tomorrow, more of the same, and then the day after we go on to Phase Two.'

'What's Phase Two?' asked Alice.

'Phase Two is when we talk about memories of happy family holidays! I'll talk to Dad about that time in Brighton. Joan, you can start getting a bit depressed. You know, a touch of the old I'm-really-gonna-miss-my-dad!'

'Check!' nodded Joan.

'I'll get Mum talking about what new outfit she's going to buy herself to go away,' said Alice. 'That should make her feel guilty.'

'Right!' said Robert. 'And remember, anything about aeroplane crashes or near-misses on the news, stare at Mum and Dad and look really, really worried!'

While this was going on, Mum and Dad were sitting in the front room, smiling at one another like a pair of crocodiles.

'Geoff Warren,' said Mum, 'you are the most conniving, underhanded, devious man I've ever met!'

'Of course!' said Dad smugly. 'That's why you married me!'

'What next?'

'Next,' said Dad, 'we can sit back and enjoy our children being polite, helpful and considerate for a few days before breaking the awful news that Granny Crump can't come and take care of them, so our plans will have to change. Then we'll take them on the holiday in the Norfolk Broads we've already booked!'

Mum laughed and shook her head.

'We are awful to our kids at times!'

Dad wagged a finger at her.

'Ah-ah!' he said. 'All's fair in love, war and families, remember?'

Mick Gowar

Mum's Best Boy

....

Tape Transcript
TOP SECRET

PROJECT DOLITTLE

Experiment: K9/1
Subject's name: Toby
Date: 1/4/92

....

(*Tape begins*) . . . Is this thing switched on yet
. . .? OK, what do I have to do . . .? (Reply
inaudible.)

Just *think*, nothing else. . .? How does it work?
How's my voice made. . .? (Reply inaudible.)

OK, *OK*! I'm sorry I asked! Look, can't you
explain it a bit simpler. . .? (Reply inaudible.)

That's fine, I get it now: a *machine*. I understand
about machines.

I'm ready now, ready to begin . . . but be

77

patient. You know, I've never done this before –
really *speak*, like a proper human being . . .'

Well, my name's Toby. I'm not sure, but I *think*
I'm about twelve years old. And at the moment I'm
sitting in a white room – like a vet's or doctor's,
only bigger, *much* bigger. All around me there are
people in long white coats, and machines –
hundreds of machines, all whirring and clicking
and buzzing.

I'm strapped to a sort of chair thing, on a raised
platform, and I've got a big metal helmet on my
head. It's got all sorts of wires and things sprouting
out of it, and there are wires stuck elsewhere on me
as well – but don't worry, it doesn't hurt a bit. In
fact, it's all the wires and machines that are letting
me speak – for the first time in my life!

What's happening to me is very important and
special. I know that because there are rows of seats
in front of me with people sitting in them: *very
important people*, all watching me and listening to
me. I can't see the people properly, because of all
the bright lights shining in my eyes, but I can see
my mum – there, at the back. She's here in case I
get frightened and need her, but I won't. I never get
frightened when Mum's with me, because I know
she'd never let anybody do anything bad to me.
Mum looks after me, and I do my best to look after
her; that's how we get along.

My mum's the most important person in my life.
Without my mum, well, I wouldn't be able to do

anything. She feeds me, baths me (not too often, because I *hate* baths), and takes me to the toilet. That's a lot, isn't it? She may look ordinary, but she's not: she's my Special Mum.

Special because she looks after me so well, and special because she picked me, know what I mean? She chose me; out of everyone in the whole world!

Well, you can see that, can't you? You can see that she's not my real mother, not the one who had me. But I don't care; she's the only mum I've ever known, and the only mum I'd ever want . . . It's just that sometimes I have these weird dreams, about her – my real mother. I was so young when I was taken from her that I can't remember what she looked like, not even in dreams; but in my dreams she's with me – like a warm body curled around me, or just the smell of her . . .

And then I wake up feeling all peculiar, and I have to get into Mum's bed for a cuddle until everything's all right again. Only Mum can do that – make things all right again.

Me and Mum, we live on our own: we don't go out much, we don't have many friends or people coming to visit. It's a quiet life, but that's the way we like it.

We listen to the radio a lot, and in the evenings we watch television. I don't like the telly much, to be honest; there's too much noise, too many bangs and too much shouting for my taste. But I like the radio, especially the music.

Sometimes, when Mum's got the radio on, I join in with the music – you know, sort of hum a bit. My voice isn't exactly what you'd call *musical*, but Mum never seems to mind.

But some people do – like the people next door! As soon as I start singing, they start banging on the wall and yelling for me to shut up.

Honestly! What a load of old miseries! I mean, where's the harm in a little sing-song? But good old Mum just takes her shoe off and bangs right back at them, and shouts: 'Go and get –' (Well, you know what I mean, don't you?)

That's another of the ways she looks after me: she stands up for me; she doesn't let people pick on me, or bully me.

You see, there are a lot of people – like the people next door – who don't like folk like me. They don't trust us; they think we might suddenly turn violent or something. It's not my singing they get cross about, not really. It's fear; prejudice – know what I mean?

Of course, they've got nothing to be afraid of: it's all a load of old rubbish, I wouldn't really hurt a fly! But don't tell *them*. I like having people a bit afraid of me. I like to have a little . . . well, *respect*. And Mum likes it too, because it helps me look after her.

Because I do look after Mum, in my own way. I'm always there when she needs someone to talk too, so she's never lonely. And she never has to answer the door on her own: I'm always there, right behind her – you know, *just in case* . . . I may be small but, like I said, people are a bit afraid of the likes of me. No one would dare try any funny business while *I'm* around!

Mind you, having people a bit scared of you can be a bit of a drag at times. Like the other day, when I decided to go out on my own for a little walk. (Well, Mum's not been too well lately, and I need to go out and get a breath of fresh air every day.)

Anyway, I nipped out – just for a minute, no more – while Mum was having a little nap. Great! It was a lovely day, and I was strolling down the High Street, minding my own business, when all of a sudden someone makes a grab for my collar – the Old Bill!

So off I go! I leg it over the road, past Tesco's and into the shopping precinct. Everything's going fine – I can see PC Plod miles behind, red in the face and wheezing like an old horse – when out of nowhere, some busybody leaps on me and holds me down until the Law finally staggers up to us.

So I have to go down to the Station, and they phone up Mum to come and get me – as usual.

Of course, there's no *law* that says I can't go out on my own the same as anybody else, is there? No. But when you're like me *they* don't need a law, because there's always some nosy-parker ready to 'have a go' – like that bloke the other day.

It's a *rule*, a secret rule: like a law, except you don't know it exists until you break it. Well, like *Grass Rules* and *House Rules* – you know what I mean, don't you?

OK, I'll explain. You know how some parks are really great – you can go wild, run around, dig up the flowers, and nobody gives a monkey's – right? And then other parks are really bad – all you've got to do is just *look* at the grass and there's some bloke in a peaked cap chasing you and screaming himself inside out? Well, *those* are Grass Rules. And the secret bit is that if you're like me, you don't know what sort of park you're in until somebody grabs you by the collar and throws you out! Now do you understand?

Well, houses can be the same: they've got House Rules, like parks, only with House Rules it can be even worse. Like, some houses I've been to you can run up and down in the hall, and jump on the furniture. Brilliant! But other places, all you've got to do is just *sniff* at some mouldy old chair and the Mum and Dad really panic: it's as if they think that any moment you're going to do something really awful – like pee on the carpet or something!

And in those kinds of houses – the bad kind – if Mum's not there, if she's left me to be looked after, they'll do dreadful things to me! I've been shut outside in the rain; I've been locked in a dark room all on my own! All because I didn't know what the stupid *rules* were!

And I've heard them talking: they think Mum does that sort of thing to me – *Mum*! But my mum would *never* do that to me! *Never! Never! Never . . .! (Sound of rapid footsteps. Tape Stops.)*

(*Tape restarts*) . . . I'm sorry. I shouldn't have. It's just that I get upset – angry, you know – with all the rules. That's how *they* get back at the likes of me, with all their rules, and all the punishments when you do something wrong. That's why I need Mum so much; to keep me safe from all that, and sometimes it worries me. Well . . . there'll come a time when she's not there any more. What will I do then, eh?

I've heard stories about what happens to folk like me when their mums have gone. I've heard that you get taken away and put into Homes, and then one morning . . . vanished! And nobody ever asks: 'Why?', 'What happened?', 'Where are they?' You just disappear, like you'd never existed.

I can tell by the way you're looking at me that it's true – isn't it? You see I'm *not* stupid, am I?

People say I'm 'dumb' – me, and others like me – 'dumb': that's what they say, isn't it? But dumb isn't the same as stupid. And I'm not even dumb, not really. It's just that I can't actually speak – not words.

But with Mum, that doesn't matter. *She* understands me. I don't know how she does it, but she knows whenever I want something – it's almost as if she could read my mind! She says she can tell from my eyes, or just from the way I'm sitting if I'm happy, or sad; if I'm hungry, or thirsty . . . anything.

Best of all, she understands how much I need to have quiet. I do; I need quiet just like I need food, or drink, or sunshine.

But a lot of people wouldn't understand that. A lot of people can't stand silence, can they? You know the sort of person I mean, don't you? They get a wild, desperate look in their eyes as soon as a room goes quiet. Then they'll come out with any old nonsense, any old jabber just as long as it fills up the silence. But my mum's not like that.

My favourite time is on winter evenings, when there isn't even the noise of traffic outside. Me and Mum sit in front of the fire. I sit at her feet, and she strokes my head and whispers to me: 'I'm the best mum in the world, and you're the best boy in the world – you're Mum's Best Boy!' It's so beautiful I'd cry if I could.

That may sound funny to you: that I could really love my mum like that, but I do. I *know* what people say about me and my kind: 'They only understand fear'; 'All they care about is their bellies'; 'They'll love anybody that feeds them'. And they'd probably think Mum was a bit mad to care for me the way she does, wouldn't they? But I'm flesh and blood, like you; I've got feelings too. There are *lots* of times when I feel real love for Mum and she feels the same for me.

Well, like that *Tree-time* – I've forgotten what it's called. You know the time I mean; when you have a tree in the living room, and lots of little pictures all round the fireplace – then. A lot of people wouldn't bother about me at that time, would they? They'd say: 'Forget about *him*. He doesn't know what it's all about. *We'll* have a good time, don't bother about *him* . . .'

But not my mum. She always buys me a present, and puts it under the tree: she even buys a present for herself and pretends it's from me!

And that makes me sad, because I'd really like to buy her a present: I'd like to do that more than anything else in the world. But I can't, can I? Even if I was able to go into a shop and ask for what I wanted, the shop people would throw me out.

They're always doing that – throwing me out of shops – even when I go in with Mum. 'Sorry, madam,' they say, 'but you can't bring *him* in here. It wouldn't be fair on the other customers; it wouldn't be hygienic.'

What a cheek! What do they think I am, a *disease* they might catch or something?

It's things like that that make me sometimes think Mum would be better off without me . . . but then, if she didn't have me, who would keep her company? Who would come round to stop her getting lonely? No one. I just wish, sometimes, that I could look after her the way she looks after me.

But the funny thing is, she doesn't seem to mind a bit that I can't do more things for her. You see, she loves me for what I am. That's pretty amazing, isn't it?

I mean, you'd think she'd want more – like . . . I dunno, a husband, or children – wouldn't you? But she doesn't: all she wants is me – that's what she says.

I've heard her telling people: 'I don't need any-body but my Toby. He's all the family I've got, and he's all the family I need. He's *the best little dog in the whole world!* He's faithful, and gentle, and he understands every word I say – don't you, Toby?'

And I do – don't I . . .? (*Tape ends.*)

Ann Pilling

Treasure Required

Anna and Jenn became friends on the school bus. They were the only people from Shemmington who went to Fletcher Middle in Ranswick. Everyone else lived in nearer villages, or in the town itself. The bus driver always grumbled about the Shemmington pick-up because the lane down to the village was so narrow and twisty.

'Bit of a dump, if you ask me,' he muttered one foggy morning as the two girls climbed on board. He'd scraped his bus on a hedge and he was in a bad mood.

'It's not a dump,' a confident little voice informed him. 'Shemmington's *historic*, it's had books written about it. You ask my mother.'

It was true, but Anna Heatherington, the new girl from London, would have been wiser keeping her mouth shut. It was only her second week on the bus and people were still making up their minds about her. New girls ought to be 'seen and not heard' according to Lindy Meyers, leader of the Class 3 gang. They always occupied the long back seat and made 'remarks' about people.

Ann Pilling

Anna had rather a posh accent and nicer clothes than a lot of the people at Fletcher Middle. She was also a very good flute player and Mrs Briggs, the music teacher, had already got her lined up for the big end of term concert. There was no Mr Heatherington, according to Jenn's mum, and Mrs was a solicitor in Ranswick. She was thin and tired-looking with permanent bags under her eyes, and she never got home from the office before seven in the evening. That's how Anna and Jenn got to know each other properly, going to each other's houses after school.

Mrs Macdonald worked late some nights too, at Fogwell's Aluminium on the industrial estate. Jenn didn't have a father either, he'd died, about the same time Anna's had walked out. So the two girls were in the same boat really, both with working mothers and dads not around any more. It was that, and the Shemmington pick-up, which had brought them together.

One morning the bus was nearly half an hour late so they passed the time reading the rows of 'For Sale and Wanted' adverts in the window of the village shop. 'Listen to this,' said Anna. 'Three dresses, size 18, one wool, one Crimplene, one corduroy.' She could mimic the flat Ranswick accent perfectly. '*Ugh*, I wouldn't like wearing someone else's cast-offs, would you, Jenn? I bet they smell funny.'

Jenn didn't answer. Some of her clothes came from a shop called Nearly New in Ranswick, and quite a few from jumble sales. It was the only way to make ends meet. Not that you could tell. Mrs Macdonald washed and mended everything beautifully. She was very fussy about things being neat and tidy and their small bungalow was always spotless.

'Treasure required,' said one postcard, 'to clean family house. Local, six hours a week, good rate of pay. Apply within.' Jenn's heart did a flip when she read it. Mum was looking for an extra job now the factory was cutting everybody's hours down. This sounded perfect.

'Nobody's replied to our ad for a cleaner yet,' Anna remarked as the school bus lurched round the corner. 'Oh heck, Happy Harry looks in a foul mood this morning. I wonder what's eating him?'

'Dunno.' Jenn wasn't really listening. If it was Mrs Heatherington's postcard then she sincerely hoped that Mum wouldn't see it. She didn't want her cleaning for Anna's mother, it would spoil things. Still, loads of village people would be after a cushy job like that. She'd never get it.

Jenn had stopped worrying about the advert long before they got off the bus. All the way to Ranswick the talk had been about the end of term concert and about Anna letting slip that she was going to play a complicated flute solo. That hadn't gone down at all well with Lindy and Co. Showing off again, that's what the new girl was doing. Jenn didn't actually hear them say it but she could tell, from their faces. They were just jealous.

She knew Mum had got the cleaning job the minute she walked into the bungalow the next afternoon because she was sitting at the kitchen table making out one of her lists: '3 p.m. to 5 p.m., Monday, Wednesdays, Fridays,' Jenn read over her shoulder. 'Clean silver alternate weeks; wash dusters Fridays; bring in bins; no polish on piano. Work phone number: Ranswick 1194.'

'Mum,' she said, flopping down on a chair, 'I don't really want you to go cleaning for Anna's mother. We're best friends now, it'll be . . . well . . . you know. Couldn't you find a job somewhere else?'

Mrs Macdonald put an arm out and squeezed Jenn's waist. 'Not easily, love, and anyway, Mrs Heatherington's really nice. She came home at lunch-time especially to interview me and gave me the job on the spot. It's a gorgeous house, the Old White Hart, it used to be a pub. I'll enjoy working there, she's got some lovely stuff.'

'But won't she want references and things?' Jenn said hopefully.

Her mother smiled. 'No. Do you know what she said to me? "Normally," she said, "I'd ask for a letter from your place of work, Mrs Macdonald, but your face is your fortune, I know I can trust you." Now, wasn't that nice?'

'*No*,' Jenn grumped, kicking her school case across the floor. 'If you ask me it was just patronizing! It's not going to work out, Mum, I just know it's not.' And she stormed off to her bedroom.

The trouble with Mum was that she was much too trusting, and only ever saw the good in people. She'd not heard Mrs Heatherington nagging Anna about her flute practice, and about getting low marks in class. She wasn't 'really nice' at all. In fact she had rather a nasty temper. Sometimes she flared up with the people at work, then had to climb down and say she was sorry. Jenn had heard all about it from Anna.

But Mrs Macdonald started cleaning at the Old White Hart the very next Monday.

'Hope you don't mind this arrangement, Jenn, between your ma and mine,' Anna said casually as they got on the bus next morning. 'My mother thinks yours is wonderful, a real treasure she calls her, just like it said on the card. She can stop worrying about the house now; I've never seen it so clean. Your mum tidies up, too. We're hopeless about putting things away.'

Yes, thought Jenn stonily. But I don't much like my mother having to pick your underwear up off the floor, or lugging your dustbins around, or cleaning your loo. Why *should* she? But she didn't say anything. Anna was her friend and this arrangement wasn't her fault. Mrs Heatherington was happy with it and Mrs Macdonald was happy with it. Everyone seemed happy except Jenn.

For a month it worked like a dream. Jenn's mum did Mrs Heatherington's cleaning while everybody was out and went home before Anna got back from school. 'It's just as if the fairies have been in,' she told Jenn enthusiastically. 'The mess used to get on Mum's nerves but she was just too tired to tackle it, at the end of the day.'

Jenn couldn't visualise a couple of fairies attacking the loo with a brush, or scrubbing acres of kitchen floor. But Mrs Macdonald actually *enjoyed* cleaning and when the Heatheringtons went away for half-term she showed Jenn proudly all over the Old White Hart.

'But won't she object?' Jenn said nervously, as they went through the various rooms. 'She's a funny woman, I think.'

'Of course not. Actually, while you're here, you could polish some silver for me.'

'Not likely!' Jenn said. 'Who do you think I am, Cinderella? I'm going home anyway.'

But before she did she followed her mother upstairs into Mrs Heatherington's bedroom. The general mess was indescribable. 'I'm not actually supposed to clean in here,' Mrs Macdonald explained. 'She's even untidier than Anna. She's always saying she'll do it herself, though I do sneak in with the duster now and then, when I've got a minute.'

'She's got some gorgeous jewellery, Mum. Look at these earrings, they must be worth a bomb.'

'They are, they're real antiques. She was left them in a will and she's just had them valued. They ought to be put away really but if I move anything she'll know I've been in here and . . . oh well, if the house gets burgled it's her business. Don't touch them, love.'

92

But Jenn rather wanted to. The earrings were solid gold, shaped like two big teardrops and inset with ovals of polished turquoise. In the middle of each was a tiny pearl. They were exquisite.

'She's bought that specially to go with them.' Mrs Macdonald pointed to a silky-looking blue dress hanging on the back of the door. 'It's for some special dinner down in London.'

'Heavens, Mum, have you seen the price label? This dress cost more than you'll earn in a year, cleaning this place. Honestly, why don't you just resign?'

'Now don't be silly, Jennifer. She can spend her money on what she likes. She works hard enough.'

'You work hard, too.'

But Mrs Macdonald ignored this. 'That old easy chair's going off to be re-covered next week,' she said evenly. 'When that's out of the way perhaps she'll let me loose in here, to do a spring clean. It could certainly do with one.'

But next week never came. On the Sunday evening a letter addressed to Mrs Audrey Macdonald was pushed through the letter-box at the bungalow. When she opened it Jenn's mum went red, then white. Then she began to cry. Jenn tore the paper from her shaking fingers and read the typed note for herself: 'Dear Mrs Macdonald, I am very sorry but, rather unexpectedly, I cannot continue with our cleaning arrangement, I enclose a week's pay but please do not trouble to come in on Monday. Perhaps you would return the key to

Anna, via Jennifer. Yours sincerely, Margaret Heatherington.'

'*Right*.' Jenn stood up. 'Come on, Mum, get your coat on, we're going straight round there. That woman's not trampling over *you*.' She felt strangely excited. Subconsciously, she'd been waiting for a chance to tell Mrs Heatherington exactly what she thought of her, getting her daughter's best friend's mother to do her charring. Anna was quite important to Jenn but, now Dad was dead, nobody mattered half as much as Mum, and here she was, dismissed and in tears.

But Mrs Macdonald refused to go, or to ring up and find out what was wrong. 'There'll be some simple explanation,' she said rather feebly. 'Perhaps she's finding the money's too much but doesn't like to say so.'

'With dresses at two hundred pounds a throw? Pull the other one, Mum,' Jenn said angrily. All right, so she couldn't drag her mother by the hair to the door of the Old White Hart, and she couldn't go herself, it was too late at night. But first thing tomorrow she'd question Anna and if that didn't produce results she'd go round to Boyd and Pringle's in Ranswick and tackle Mrs Heatherington in her office.

Anna didn't say a word while they waited for the bus but as soon as it left Shemmington Jenn pitched straight in. 'What's your mother sacked

Mum for?' she said. 'I suppose you know about this?' And she held up the letter.

The other girl turned scarlet. 'I'm . . . I'm not supposed to discuss it, Jenn,' she stammered. 'Please don't ask me to. It's awful. She's lost those gold earrings that Aunty Winifred left her, and we've been away, and she thinks –'

For a minute Jenn couldn't get the words out. Then she said, 'She thinks that Mum's *stolen* them? Is that it?' Her voice was loud and harsh, and everybody on the bus was listening. Anna stared out of the window and a big tear rolled down her cheek. 'I've told her it's ridiculous,' she sobbed, 'but she's just in one of her stupid moods, won't listen to anybody. My father's sent her a nasty letter, about money or something, and it's really upset her. Then old Mr Pringle phoned from the office and complained about a case she's handling, then she couldn't find the earrings. Everything's got on top of her, Jenn.'

'So she wrote and more or less accused my mother of being a thief?'

'Listen, I know perfectly well they'll turn up. If you could just calm down . . .' But Jenn had already gone to sit with Lindy Meyers and Co. on the back seat.

By break everybody in 3B knew that Anna Heatherington's crazy mother was accusing Jenn's mum of stealing her jewellery and that Mrs Macdonald was just sitting down under the treatment. Everyone liked a scandal and Jenn became wildly popular overnight. Most people stopped speaking to the new girl.

Jenn hated the whole thing. She was angry with Anna's mum for over-reacting, angry with her own for being so meek and mild. And she missed Anna's friendship. This affair was nothing to do with them, yet it had parted them. Most breaks and lunch-times Anna went off to the music block to practise for the concert. It was less painful for both of them that way.

Every day Jenn pleaded with her mother to go and tackle Mrs Heatherington and she had no doubt that Anna was trying to talk sense into hers too, at the other end of the village. But Mrs Macdonald was quietly stubborn. She'd done nothing wrong and that would 'come out in the end', she said. Meanwhile, she was looking in the village shop again, for another job.

One Sunday night, just three weeks after the letter, there was a knock on the front door. Jenn opened it and found Mrs Heatherington on the step. No sign of Anna, just the tall thin solicitor, her face drawn tight with nerves, her eyes rather pink. 'Is your mother in?' she said.

Jenn asked her to come inside then fetched Mum. Very soon the front-room door had closed firmly on the two of them with Jenn on the outside. For a minute she debated whether to stay and listen. She didn't but, as she went off down the hall, she definitely heard Mrs Heatherington burst into tears. It was quite loud, even through the closed door.

They were in there together for nearly an hour. Jenn fiddled about in the kitchen with the door propped open, in case she missed something. But when Mrs Heatherington left she went very quickly, only pausing to bend down and give Mrs Macdonald a kiss. 'And thank you, thank you so much, Audrey,' Jenn heard, as she went off down the path.

'Well, so what was all that about?' Mum had come into the kitchen and was filling the kettle. Her eyes were a bit watery too, now. 'She wouldn't stop for a cup of tea,' she said, 'but I certainly feel like one.'

'It's "Audrey" now, I notice,' Jenn muttered sarcastically. 'Go on then, what did she say?'

'Only that she was sorry. Remember that tatty old chair in her bedroom? Well, a man in Ranswick's re-upholstering it for her. He stripped it this afternoon and found those earrings down the back. Don't ask me how they got there. I suppose it's because the poor woman lives in such a muddle. Anyhow, they've turned up, that's the main thing.'

'But it's *not*, Mum,' Jenn exploded. 'Poor woman, my foot. She accused you of taking them, *you*. And she sacked you. I bet you could take her to court for that. You could use a solicitor on her. That'd be a laugh.'

'Now listen, Jenn, I don't want to hear that kind of talk, if you don't mind. It was a misunderstanding and we've sorted it out. She's been under a lot of strain lately and she wasn't thinking straight. That's how these things happen. That ex-husband's been writing her nasty letters for one thing. It's no fun being left on your own. We know that, don't we?'

There was a sudden silence in the kitchen, the silence that always came when they were thinking about Dad. Then Jenn said, 'Well, don't dare tell me that you're going back to work for her because if you are I'm moving out.'

'We didn't discuss that, Jenn. She just came round to say she was sorry. I admire her for doing that. Some people would have written.

'And by the way,' she added, when she got no reply, 'be a bit nicer to Anna. I hear the whole form's ignoring her now, and all because of a silly mix-up. It wasn't her fault.'

'No, and it wasn't yours.'

'Jenn, it was *nobody's* fault. Now, do you want this cup of tea or don't you?'

Lindy Meyers had managed to get Mrs Briggs to let her help with seating arrangements for the school concert, and she'd done her job well. Anna and Jenn were friends again, in a shy, hesitant sort of way, but Lindy and Co. were still putting the boot in.

When Mrs Heatherington arrived she was shown to a seat at the front because she was the mother of a soloist, but nobody else was given a place on her row. She sat alone and ignored in her dark grey suit, tight-lipped and white-faced, pointedly studying her programme while the gossipy whispers went on around her.

Jenn and her mum nearly missed the concert because the bus broke down. 'There are two good seats here, Mrs Macdonald,' Lindy said, pushing at them officiously.

'Er, thanks, dear, but I'd rather be nearer the front if you don't mind. Come on, Jenn, there's plenty of room in Mrs Heatherington's row.'

Anna's solo was the glory of the concert, a sad and beautiful piece from an opera, called "The Dance of the Blessed Spirits". In the story, the programme explained, Orpheus goes down to Hell to try and rescue his dead wife Eurydice. All the pain and loss of parting was in the melancholy sound of the little silver flute.

As she listened the tears poured down Mrs Heatherington's face. Jenn's mum quietly stretched out an arm and took the long thin hand into her own little red chapped one, holding it firmly there till the music and the crying were over.

Jan Mark

Dan, Dan, the Scenery Man

The first time June saw Dad on stage she was only six and she did not recognize him. The play had been about Noah's Ark and June had gone along with Mum hoping to see the animals come in two by two. Instead it was just people in bedspreads who spent most of their time sitting round a table, arguing. Dad turned up in the middle of one fierce row as a bent old man wearing a thin white beard, and even when Mum nudged her and hissed, 'There's Daddy,' June could hardly believe it. They went home straight after the performance and Dad came in about an hour later, tall, upright, young again, but his chin looked red and sore where the beard had come off.

The village dramatic society staged a panto- mime every Christmas. This year it was *Dick Whittington*. Dad never really acted, he said he preferred to be backstage, and still only appeared in what he called 'walk-on parts' in which he did just that; walked on and later walked off again.

But he went to the village hall every Friday evening and at weekends disappeared into the garden shed where he built London Bridge and the Sultan's palace out of hardboard. His friend Simon, who was playing Alderman Fitzwarren, came along to help and in between sawing and hammering, Dad heard his lines. Sometimes Simon broke into song, ditties about diddling and fiddling and financial scandals. Mum said she supposed it would sound funny on the night.

'Why don't you join the society?' June asked her. Dad had abandoned that suggestion long ago.

'I've got something better to do with my time,' Mum said, regularly. She always did the ironing on Friday nights, as if to prove that she had no time for play-acting. 'Anyway,' she added, 'I can't act.'

'Nor can most of them,' June said. She did a lot of drama at school these days, and knew that there was more to acting than pretending to be somebody else. You had to turn yourself into somebody else, be them and think for them, even if it were for only a few minutes at a time. The society members looked impressive on stage, very at-home and confident, but watching from the dark of the village hall she could never forget that they were Mr Sleaman the dentist, Mrs Elsenham who ran the Cub Scouts, the estate agent, Simon from up the road. Very few of them could disappear inside someone else's skin as soon as they stepped out from the wings. Mrs Elsenham played pretty young girls, but you never lost sight of Mrs

Elsenham who was pretty, but not a girl, and rather gathered about the neck, like a draw-string bag. In the pantomine she was Alderman Fitzwarren's daughter Alice.

'Simon's *daughter*?' Mum said, when Dad told them. 'She's old enough to be his mother!'

'Sister,' Dad protested, mildly. Mum was at that moment very busy with housework, as she always was when Dad mentioned the dramatic society. But June loved hearing about rehearsals. She longed to join the society herself when she was old enough. Children were sometimes borrowed for special occasions, particularly the pantomimes, when fairies or small animals were required. This year there was to be a rat ballet, which danced about teasing Dick Whittington's cat. June had known better than to ask if she could audition for it. Dad would have liked her to.

She was in bed when he came home from rehearsals, although she always heard him slam the front gate. Anything he wanted to tell her had to wait till breakfast next day, so it was one Saturday morning, at the beginning of December, when he came into the kitchen and said, 'We've got a bit of a crisis on our hands.'

'What's a crisis?' June asked. 'Like on the news?'

'It means the Good Fairy has developed a septic toe,' Mum said grimly.

'We don't have a Good Fairy in *Dick Whittington*,' Dad said.

'It was a septic toe last year. Anyone would

think her leg had dropped off, the fuss you all made.'

'Well, she did have a lot of dancing to do. No, we've actually *lost* a dancer, this time.'

'Went down the plughole, I suppose.'

'The Malones are going away for Christmas.'

'I didn't think they belonged.' Mr and Mrs Malone sang in the choral society, in evening dress. It was hard to imagine them banging about at the village hall wearing false beards and fishnet tights.

'They don't, but little Zara belongs to the dancing class and she was our solo rat. She does – did – a dance in front of the curtain while the senior rats do a quick change into belly-dancers for scene three.'

'That's a crisis,' Mum said to June, witheringly.

'What I thought was . . .' Dad said, and then he seemed to think again. 'You're doing Christmas things at school now, aren't you? Not much work?'

June nodded. They were right in the middle of that lovely break-down in routine that went on until they broke up; post boxes, decorations, carols in assembly, the Nativity Play, in which she, like Dad, had a walk-on part; always a shepherd, never the Virgin Mary.

'What's all this?' Mum's mouth went tight and suspicious. Nativity Plays were all right, unavoidable even. Everyone had them, like Income Tax demands, but they both knew that Dad had something else in mind.

'I was thinking of that butterfly dance you did at the school concert. You could still do it, couldn't you? You haven't forgotten it?'

'A butterfly instead of a rat?' June said.

Mum said, 'Dick Whittington's cat didn't hunt butterflies, come off it, Keith.'

'The same dance, only dressed as a rat – the costume Zara wears would fit you. And, as I recall, it might just as well have been a rat last time, except for the wings. Not that it wasn't very nice,' he added, hurriedly, 'but it wasn't all that much like butterflies.'

'You mean, I could be in the panto and go to rehearsals?' She spoke to Dad but she looked at Mum.

'And come home at half-past eleven?' Mum said. 'Don't be silly.'

'We'd come straight home at ten,' Dad said. 'And there's only a couple more evening rehearsals before she breaks up; *Friday* evenings . . . no falling asleep in class.'

'It's not to become a habit,' Mum said.

'How could it?'

'Not a regular thing –'

'A one-off. Promise.' If only he wouldn't wheedle. 'I just thought it might be fun for her.'

Half the fun was in looking forward to it, spreading the news at school, telling snooty Zara Malone that she would be stepping into her role.

'You're welcome,' Zara informed her. 'I didn't

want to be a rat anyway. You wait till you put that smelly old mask on.'

'I have,' June said. She had tried out the costume the night before. 'It smells of you. *Eau de Malone.* Yuk!' They were separated by the headmaster before June could return Zara's kick. Her ankle was sore all day but she was too pleased with the *Eau de Malone* crack to care.

Rehearsals began at seven-thirty. At seven o'clock it was already a stone-cold night, still, silent, beaded with stars, as June and Dad walked over the level crossing, through the council estate and up the hill to the village hall. From far away they could see the three long windows shining warmly like lanterns above the houses.

Once inside, away from the black night, the icy stars, June noticed how thin and chill the light really was, how the air smelled of dust and cigar-ette smoke, but the magic was working already. At one end of the hall was the stage, a box filled with golden glow, and on it Dad's scenery, no longer bits of deal and hardboard but Highgate Hill, where Dick heard the bells of London calling him back to become Lord Mayor; and there was the milestone where he sat to rest, and beyond it the backdrop; London as it must have looked hundreds of years ago; red roofs and steeples gathered round the high dome of St Paul's, and never a tower block in sight. Beside the milestone, sleeves rolled up, a clipboard under his arm, stood Mr Sleaman, the dentist. Without his white smock he looked wild and unreliable as he ran his fingers through his hair and made furious gestures to the Vicar who was up a step-ladder at the side of the hall, wrestling with a spotlight. When he saw Dad he waved his flailing arms and called, 'Hello, Dan! What do you think of it?'

Dad waved back. 'Great stuff, Tom, though I say it myself!' Mr Sleaman's name really was Tom, but Dad was called Keith. June was just about to ask him why he answered to Dan, but he gently shunted her forward. 'Tom, meet our replacement rat.'

Mr Sleaman vaulted lightly down from the stage, rushed over to June, shook her hand, cried madly that she was an angel, and swarmed up the ladder where he collided with the Vicar who was swarming down, like a pirate descending from the rigging with a spanner in his teeth.

'If I were you,' Dad said, 'I'd just sit down somewhere quietly and watch until we call you.'

He flung off his duffle-coat, pushed up his sleeves and dived through a door at the side of the stage.

A voice on the other side of it shrieked, 'Dan! Darling! *When* are you going to fix this flat? It simply *flaps* every time I open the window.' June knew the voice. She had last heard it at that volume in July, at the village fête, marshalling Cub Scouts for a gymnastic display. Dad bobbed out from behind a tree on the stage.

'Have no fear, Dan is here,' he hollered, whipping out a screwdriver. June gazed. What was the matter with him?

All round her people were taking off coats and unwinding scarves to pile on the stacking chairs that lined the sides of the hall. Every few seconds a blast of cold air scoured her legs as someone flounced in from the darkness and dragged the door shut. No one walked or spoke. They skipped, dodged, hit each other on the back, while laughing, shouting, squealing. Six woman-sized girls from the dancing class – the ones who were doubling as rats and belly-dancers – slipped off their coats to reveal hairy body stockings, and began to limber up, swinging their legs dangerously. On all sides people called for Tom, the director, Sparks – who was the Vicar – or Dan – who was Dad. Everyone wanted Dan. Mrs Elsenham was struck on the chin by the soaring hind leg of a belly-dancing rat. June heard the Vicar say damn, twice.

At half-past seven, when the rehearsal was due to begin, they all looked as if they had been there for hours. Tom danced into the middle of the mob and clapped his hands. 'All right, troupers! Let's start with a quick run-through of scenes two and three so we can see how our new little rat shapes up.' He made a magnificent gesture in June's direction. Every head turned toward her and people clapped.

'Dan's girl,' a voice said.

'Does her mother know she's out?' said another. Both voices laughed and June felt uneasy, but after a moment there was a kind of restless hush and on to the stage walked Dad's mate Simon. He turned to the front, rubbed his hands and said, 'Just off to the Stock Exchange. I think I'll put in a spot of insider-dealing before lunch.' There was something odd about Simon. June saw him often enough in the shed, with Dad, and he always had a part in the plays – but he didn't quite seem to be acting. On the other hand, he wasn't the nice, ordinary Simon who came round on Saturdays, any more than the Vicar seemed to be the Vicar, or Mrs Elsenham, the cub mistress. And if June had never seen Tom Sleaman before, she would not have dreamed of allowing him anywhere near her teeth.

Mrs Elsenham was, without doubt, the battiest of the lot, tripping about with a floaty scarf that snagged on the scenery so that 'Darling Tom' or 'Darling Simon' or 'Darling Dan' had to rush on stage and unhook her. Dan was everywhere, efficient, dependable Dan. Each time somebody fussed or complained – Mrs Elsenham was in tears at one point and wailed that she could not go on – Tom Sleaman or the Vicar would say, 'Dan will see to it . . . Make a note of that, Dan,' and the fuss would subside.

The rat solo was a success, no one could have guessed that it had started out as a butterfly. As June appeared on stage alone – while the other rats changed into belly-dancers, swapping their tails and whiskers for harem pants and spangled bras –

there was no need to rehearse with anyone else except Dick Whittington's cat who worked at the estate agent's and came creeping round the curtains at the end to chase her into the wings. People applauded kindly and Mrs Elsenham, lurking backstage, swatted her with a damp kiss and said she was a natural. June supposed that was a compliment.

The rehearsal ran late and it was almost ten before June and Dad got away. The others were straggling off to the Black Prince, for a post mortem, they said, which June had thought was something you did with corpses.

'Don't you want to go with them?' June said. Now she understood why Dad came home at eleven-thirty on Fridays.

'Not tonight,' he said, and tucked her arm into his. 'I'm seeing my girl home.'

They walked down the hill where the pavements glittered with frost.

'Dad?'

'Mmm?'

'Why do they call you Dan?'

'It started as a joke,' he said. 'Somebody called me Dan, Dan, the Scenery Man, and it stuck.'

She said, 'Is that why you pretend . . .?' and tailed off, not quite sure what she had meant to ask.

'I don't pretend.'

'But you aren't like that really.'

'What do you mean by really?' Dad said. 'Think

what I do for a living: sell shoes. I don't have to be Dan, Dan, the Scenery Man in Dolcis, do I? I couldn't be.'

'You aren't like that at home.'

'We don't need Dan at home, either,' Dad said. 'Your mum sees to all that.'

'Are you acting, then?'

'I can't act. If I could, I wouldn't be doing the scenery, would I?'

They walked on, through the council estate. There were already Christmas trees in some of the windows.

'But you were all being different, weren't you?'

'How long do you think Mrs E. would last with the cubs if she went on like that? We're just being ourselves,' he said, 'but you're right, in a way; different selves.'

'Like – acting being actors?'

'And electricians, and scenery men. Maybe Sparks really is an electrician, and only acts being a vicar. Acting isn't just pretending, is it?'

They had to wait at the level crossing for the ten-twenty from Ashford to trundle into the station.

'Do you like being Dan, Dan, the Scenery Man?'

'Better than selling shoes, to tell the truth.'

June looked up at his face, lit in flashes from the passing train.

'Aren't you happy?' She pressed his arm. She had not thought before that he might not be.

'Not all the time. Are you?'

'No . . . not *happy*.'

'Of course not.' The crossing barriers rose slowly, like curtains swept aside. They moved forward. 'I can't say you'll grow out of it because you're just growing into it.'

'Into what?'

'Well . . .' He seemed unsure. 'Just growing up, really. You don't change, as you get older, but you learn to *seem* different when you need to, when you want to be.'

They were almost home. 'Mum doesn't,' June said. 'She's always the same.'

'How do you know? How do you know what she's like when you're not there – when she isn't being Mum. What do you think she's doing now?'

'Ironing,' June said, her hand on the gate.

'No – don't open it. Sssh! Wait.' Dad silently stepped over their low garden wall and beckoned June to follow. 'Walk on the grass,' he whispered. 'Now, come round to the side.'

The heavy brown curtains were drawn across the bay window of the living room, but the little side window was hung with net. June and Dad crept towards it and peered through. Inside Mum was sitting on the settee with her shoes off and her feet drawn up. The biscuit tin was open beside her, and a coffee cup was balanced on the arm of the settee; something she would never allow June to do for fear of spillage. The television was on, through the glass they could hear lush romantic music. Dad looked down at June, raised his eyebrows and slipped away across the dark garden. A moment later she heard the gate open and then slam, and she ran round to the front to meet Dad as he crunched slowly up the gravel path.

When he opened the front door there was no sound of music from the telly; instead they heard the unmistakeable clang of the tubular steel ironing board being folded up in the kitchen. Mum came out to meet them with a stack of sheets in her arms.

'Have a good time?' she asked, wearily.

'June's a star in the making,' Dad said, and for a second she could almost hear Dan, Dan, the Scenery Man. 'Look, you sit down. We'll make some coffee. Put the kettle on, Rat Woman!'

June went into the kitchen. The biscuit tin stood on the working surface, beside the iron, and the coffee cup was draining on the washing-up rack. As she stood, waiting for the kettle to boil, she touched her finger to the iron. It was quite cold.

Tony Bradman

You're Late, Dad

Steven's classroom was at the front of the school, and his desk was next to the window. So, just by turning his head slightly, he could see most of the street outside.

It was almost lunch-time, and they were supposed to be doing silent reading. But Steven couldn't concentrate on his book, even though it was a good one. He couldn't stop thinking about the afternoon. It was Sports Day and he knew, he just *knew* that he was going to win a race. And Dad had promised to be there.

Steven looked up. Mr Brooks was marking a huge pile of exercise books with a frown on his face. It was very quiet. All Steven could hear was the sound of Mr Brooks picking up exercise books and slapping them down again, and Samantha's wheezy breathing close behind him.

Samantha had asthma, so she couldn't be in any races. But she sat next to Nicky, who was the fastest runner in the school, or so everyone said.

He *was* fast, but Steven knew he was going to beat him today. He could see the end of the race in his mind, in slow motion, just the way it was on the TV. He'd burst through the tape, Nicky miles behind him, and Dad would be right there, cheering him on. It was going to be great. No it wasn't . . . it was going to be amazing!

Out of the corner of his eye, Steven saw something moving in the street. He turned quickly, but carefully, so no one would notice, and saw a car stop. But it was a red Metro, not Dad's dark blue Ford. It was too early for him to arrive yet, anyway. Sports Day didn't start till two o'clock.

Steven just hoped he wasn't going to be late this time.

Steven's dad looked at his watch and swore under his breath. It was nearly twelve . . . where had the morning gone? He'd got nothing done, even though he'd been frantically busy from the moment he'd sat down at his desk. The phone hadn't stopped ringing, so he hadn't even made a start on that report. And it was supposed to be finished today.

He did some quick mental arithmetic. If he started it now, right now, he could probably finish it in an hour or so. It would take him five minutes to get to the car park, then half an hour to get to the school. He smiled to himself. There was plenty of time.

He pulled a pad towards him from the mess of

papers on his desk, picked up his pen, and thought. A sentence began to form itself in his mind, but evaporated when the phone rang.

'Hello, Jim Morris speaking,' he said.

'Hello, Jim, Bob Daniels here.'

Jim sat up straight in his chair. Bob Daniels was his boss, and a very important man.

'Could you come over to my office for a meeting this afternoon, Jim? About three o'clock?'

Jim explained that he had already asked for the afternoon off to go to his son's Sports Day.

'Oh yes, I remember now . . .' said Bob Daniels. He paused. 'That's a bit of a nuisance, Jim.'

Jim knew the boss wasn't pleased about it. Bob Daniels liked his employees to do what *he* wanted, and show him what wonderful workers they were. He didn't think they should have time off for things like Sports Days.

'Can't your wife go instead?' he was saying. 'This *is* very important.'

'That's impossible, I'm afraid,' said Jim curtly. He was cross now . . . Bob Daniels knew he was divorced.

'Well, pop in and see me before you go. I'd like a chat . . .'

Jim said he would, and put the phone down. He looked at his watch, then started writing very fast.

Steven picked at his food. He was too excited to eat, and besides, he didn't really like macaroni cheese. He pushed his plate away.

'Are you leaving all that?' said Nicky, who was

sitting opposite him. 'I'll have it if you don't want it.'

Steven said OK, and soon Nicky was scooping leftovers into his mouth as fast as he could go. Steven tried to concentrate on his yoghurt, but his eyes kept drifting back to the lumps of macaroni cheese disappearing into Nicky.

'Is your mum coming this afternoon?' Nicky said between mouthfuls. He didn't wait for an answer. 'Mine is, and my dad said he'd be there too . . .'

Steven let Nicky's voice wash over him. Nicky's mum and dad would definitely be there, with his little brother, his baby sister, his granny and grandpa, an aunt or two, and even the dog, probably. His entire family always seemed to come to everything at the school, whatever it was, whenever it happened.

Steven's mum came to the school sometimes. She'd managed to get the afternoon off from her job for the Harvest Festival, and for the Christmas Concert. And when the headmistress had written to her about his school work, and how he needed to pull up his socks, she had come in to see her the very next morning.

But Steven's dad hadn't been to the school for years, not since before the divorce.

At first his mum wouldn't let him see Steven at all. Then they'd come to an agreement, and Dad was allowed to take him out on a Saturday. He was supposed to arrive at ten-thirty and bring

Steven back at one o'clock. But he was always late. Most Saturdays Steven spent ages standing at the window . . . waiting.

It hadn't mattered so much at first. Then Steven's mum got the job in the shop, and had to work on Saturday mornings. Dad was supposed to pick Steven up at nine-thirty now. She got really angry when he was late, as he was every week, without fail.

Last Saturday they had stood arguing in the street with Steven standing between them. He had closed his eyes and remembered all the nights he'd spent lying in bed, listening to his parents shout and fight downstairs.

He didn't miss all that. But he did miss Dad, although he never told Mum how he felt. She didn't like talking about Dad or the divorce, and Steven didn't want to upset her. They got on OK most of the time, and underneath it all she was still the same old Mum. But she was always so busy these days, and when she wasn't busy she was tired. And she hardly ever smiled.

Dad didn't do much smiling either. He lived in a poky little flat on the other side of town, and Steven knew he hated taking him there on a Saturday. That was why they spent most of their time together in the park, or at MacDonalds, or driving out into the country to see the sights they'd seen a million times before.

When his mum told Dad how difficult it was to get an afternoon off for Sports Day, Steven's heart had sunk. There would be no one there to cheer him on. And then Dad had said *he* would come. Steven had been amazed – and really, really pleased.

'I'll believe it when I see it,' his mum had said as she'd marched off down the street to work. But his Dad had promised.

'Don't you worry, son,' he'd said. 'I'll be there.'

Nicky was eating an apple now, and still talking. Steven looked beyond him at the clock on the wall. It was one-twenty. He wondered where his dad was, right at that moment.

The lift wasn't working, so Jim ran down the stairs as fast as he could. By the time he got to the bottom, seven floors below his office, he was taking them three at a time. He swung round the bannister at the end, and ran towards the main doors, nearly knocking the security man over as he shot out.

He was right in the middle of the shopping centre. Today it seemed as if everyone within one hundred miles had come in to shop. Jim could hardly get through the crowds. It usually only took him five minutes to reach the car park, but at this rate he'd be lucky if he ever got there at all.

He tried to run, dodging past the old-age pensioners, the mums with pushchairs, bumping into people and shouting sorry over his shoulder. It was a warm day, and soon he could feel the sweat dripping off his forehead. His shirt stuck to his back, and his suit jacket felt as if it weighed a ton.

It was Bob Daniels' fault that he was late. Jim had gone to see him on his way out, and had been treated to a little lecture about how his work had been suffering, how he needed to pull up his socks if he wanted to get on . . . All he'd wanted to do by then was to get out, but you can't really hurry your boss when he's giving you a telling off. He'd just let the words wash over him in the end. He knew he wasn't doing his best at work, and he worried about it. Money had been really tight since the divorce, and it was getting harder just to make ends meet. The last thing he needed was to lose his job.

Barbara was right, though; it wasn't fair that she should be the one to go to Steven's school all the time. But she didn't seem to realise how difficult it was to explain things to a boss like Bob Daniels. It always ended in a row when they talked about it, and Steven hated them rowing. Sometimes he felt as if he was hardly part of Steven's life any more, but he didn't know what to do about it. Nothing was easy now. Everything was a mess.

Jim ran into the car park. His car was on the fifth floor, but the lift there wasn't working either, so he turned to go up the dark, dirty, graffiti-covered stairway. He stopped to get his breath back, and looked at his watch. It was one-thirty-three. He had a sudden vision of his son's face wearing a look of complete disappointment.

'I'll make it, Steven,' he said aloud as he ran up

the first flight. 'I *swear* I'll make it.'

'I don't think your dad's going to make it,' said Nicky. Steven didn't say anything. He just kept his eyes fixed on the street beyond the fence around the school playing fields. He wasn't sure, but he thought his dad would have to come that way when he finally arrived. If he ever got there.

'He'll make it,' he said.

'You can always come and stand with us while you wait,' said Nicky. He waved in the direction of his family, a large group of people standing nearby. There were lots of small children with them, as well as several dogs, and they were all laughing and making a lot of noise. Steven didn't reply.

'Suit yourself,' said Nicky. He walked off, and Steven watched him go. He wished now that he hadn't said anything about his dad coming, but it had all spilled out while they were getting changed. Nicky had been going on about his dad, and how he'd been a really great runner when he was at school.

'My dad was a good runner too,' Steven had said. And before he could stop himself, he was saying all sorts of things about his dad that weren't true, about how he'd been a brilliant runner and won loads of cups and medals. Nicky had looked as if he didn't believe him, which only made Steven say even more.

But now it was nearly two o'clock, and there

was no sign of Dad anywhere. He was going to be late, that was for sure, but Steven had half expected that. It wouldn't matter so long as he got there before the big race, the four hundred metres, and that wasn't until two-thirty. So there was still time.

'Starters for the first race, please!' Mr Brooks called out. A gaggle of children surrounded him. 'Not all at once, not all at once,' he shouted crossly, and began handing out coloured bibs with numbers on.

Steven looked towards the street again.

'Come on, Dad,' he whispered. 'Where *are* you?'

Jim drummed his fingers on the steering wheel. The car in front hadn't moved for the last five minutes, and as far ahead as he could see there was a long line of cars, all well and truly stuck in a traffic jam.

He just couldn't believe it. It had taken him nearly ten minutes to get out of the car park, and another ten to get on to the bypass. Now here he was on what was supposed to be the fast route – and he wasn't moving at all.

He should have cut across town . . . it couldn't have been any slower. He daren't look at his watch. He knew he was late, and he didn't want to know *how* late any more.

Suddenly the car in front started moving, and soon the line of cars was edging slowly along. Jim sat up in his seat and tried to see what was happening. Four or five cars ahead the line was slowing to a stop again. But just then, he saw an 'Exit' sign coming upon his left.

'Right,' he said aloud. He sat back in his seat, swung the steering wheel over hard, and hit the accelerator. He shot away with a squeal of tyres, raced into the exit slip road and headed for town.

'Nothing's going to beat me today,' he whispered as the engine roared. He was determined to make it. 'Nothing . . .'

'Right,' said Mr Brooks. 'Starters for the four hundred metres, fourth-year boys. Come on, we haven't got all day!'

Steven and the others in the race took their numbered bibs from him. There were eight of them altogether, and Steven was number three, Nicky number two. So they'd be next to each other.

'Line up now,' Mr Brooks was saying. Steven found his lane, and stood while the others found theirs.

'Come on, Nicky!' someone called from the crowd at the side of the track. Other voices joined in. 'You can do it, Nicky! You can do it!' Nicky smiled and waved, then clasped his hands and raised them over his head like a champion.

Steven looked away, towards the street. There was no sign of a dark blue Ford, no sign of his dad. He wasn't going to make it. He wouldn't be there. He'd broken his promise.

'To your marks please, boys,' Mr Brooks said. The eight boys were now in their lanes, poised, waiting for the start. Steven looked down at the toe of his trainer on the white line just in front of him. He could hear a buzz of voices, then everything seemed to go quiet. His throat felt tight, and his eyes were prickling.

A tear ran down his cheek and fell on a white-painted blade of grass. It made the white run.

'Ready . . . steady . . .'

There was a bang, and Steven was running.

Jim swung the car round the corner and squealed to a halt in the first space he could see. One of the front wheels hit the curb with a clunk, and he knew without looking that the back of the car was sticking well out into the road. But he didn't care.

He flung open the door, jumped out and started running past the school fence. He could hear a crowd cheering and calling names, and as he looked he could see some children running round the track on the playing fields.

He came to the school gates at last, and ran through. He didn't stop, but ran straight on, past the main building, past the playground, past the infants sitting in a group with their teachers, past the headmistress and the head of the board of governors who both stared at him open-mouthed, and right up to the winning line . . .

. . . Just as two boys came off the last bend and

headed for the tape. They were neck and neck, each straining to get in front of the other.

Steven could feel Nicky right next to him. He could hear voices calling Nicky's name, he could feel his legs getting tired, his heart beating as if it was going to explode, his lungs bursting. He wasn't going to make it.

'Come on, Steven!' Someone was calling out *his* name. 'Come on, Steven, you can do it!'

There wasn't far to go now. Steven could see the tape, and standing beyond it he could see his dad. He ran, he ran as fast as he could. He burst through the tape and into his dad's arms.

At first neither of them could speak. They were both out of breath, puffing and panting and holding on to each other. Out of the corner of his eye, Steven could see Nicky's mum and dad walking off with him, their arms round his shoulders. Nicky looked back at him, but Steven didn't care about anything or anyone else.

He freed a hand to wipe his eyes, then stepped back and looked up at his dad.

'Steven, I . . .' Jim started to say.

'You're late, Dad,' said Steven, but he smiled as he said it. His dad smiled back, then put an arm round Steven's shoulder. They walked off together towards the others.

The Authors

Michelle Magorian writes: 'One afternoon while waiting for a dance class, I spotted two young people in a studio among the Adult Ballet students. White and black, they were talking in animated fashion at the barre as they limbered up. Their enthusiasm led me to the story, "The Greatest".'

Michelle Magorian is best known for her award-winning novel, *Goodnight Mister Tom*.

Hazel Townson, author of 'Scarecrows', writes: 'Vivid memories of my own childhood drove this story into print. I was constantly being exhorted to keep myself tidy, and the pockets of my coats were sewn up so that I couldn't possibly drag them out of shape by stuffing my hands or possessions in them. My most popular book is *The Speckled Panic*, about toothpaste which turns out to be Truthpaste, guaranteed to make you tell the truth for up to twenty-four hours after use.'

Trish Cooke, author of 'Grow Up, Maxine', writes: 'I was inspired to write this story after looking closely at the behaviour of my ten-year-old niece after the divorce of her parents. It was very apparent that an 'attitude' was developing. I therefore dedicate this story to Mel, whose attitude is constantly changing as her eyes open wider and realisation creeps in.'

Trish Cooke has just published her first book, *Mammy Sugar Falling Down*. She is also a regular presenter on BBC TV's *Playbus*.

Brian Morse writes: 'I hope Don, Jane's dad, will forgive me for "Flooding the Sahara". I visited them while they barged their way round the Birmingham canals last summer. This disaster seemed just up their street. I write poems and novels for all age-groups. My best-known book, *Breaking Glass*, is a Puffin Plus for teenagers.'

Jenny Nimmo lives in Wales with her painter husband and three children. She has just completed the prizewinning *Snow Spider* trilogy (*The Snow Spider*, *Emlyn's Moon* and *The Chestnut Soldier*) which tells the story of Gwyn, who is given five gifts on his ninth birthday to see if he is a magician – gifts which land him in the most fantastic adventures. *The Snow Spider* was dramatised for television and first shown last Christmas.

Andrew Matthews, author of 'Love, War and Families', writes: 'I wanted to write a story in which two parents were as good at getting their own way as their children. I'm the youngest of four sons. By the time I came along, my parents knew just what to expect and how to handle it. They still do!'

The Authors

Andrew Matthews' most recent book is *Dr Monsoon Taggert's Amazing Finishing Academy*, and is published by Methuen Children's Books.

Mick Gowar writes: ' "Mum's Best Boy" is loosely based on the neighbours we had when I was a boy. I was born and brought up in Pinner, and the road my family lived in was a very 'doggy road'. It seemed to be full of elderly ladies walking small yappy dogs. If you listened carefully, you could sometimes over-hear them talking to their dogs: "Hurry up, there's a good boy – Mummy's waiting . . . Don't sniff that, or Mummy will be *very* angry!" As if the dogs were children; which in a sense they *were*. "Mum's Best Boy" is my idea of what might happen if one of those child/dogs was suddenly able to speak.'

Mick Gowar is a well-known poet, and author of *Third Time Lucky* (Viking Kestrel) and *Swings and Roundabouts* (Fontana).

Ann Pilling's 'Treasure Required' explores a theme which has always interested her: how circumstance can throw together people of widely differing backgrounds, and expect them to 'get on'. She feels children suffer particularly from private social arrangements forced on them by their parents. Simple misunderstanding can cause heartache, another theme which has always preoccupied this writer; but compassionate forgiveness can resolve it, as the story shows.

The Authors

The complexities of human relationships are fully explored in two recent books, *On the Lion's Side* and *Stan*. Ann is probably best known for *Henry's Leg* which won the 1986 *Guardian* Award and became a best-seller.

Jan Mark, author of 'Dan, Dan, the Scenery Man', writes: 'I once belonged to a dramatic society for a short while. It was much more highbrow than the one I've written about here, and never stooped to anything so low as a pantomime (that was another dramatic society that I *didn't* belong to), but like the one in my own story, most of the acting took place off-stage.'

Jan Mark has written many popular books for children, among them *Handles* and *Trouble Half-Way*.

Tony Bradman, author of 'You're Late, Dad', writes: 'The idea for this story came from my own childhood. My parents were divorced, and I remember vividly waiting for my father to arrive on Saturday mornings to take me out. He was supposed to come and see me running in a race on Sports Day once, and he was very late . . . My best-known books are the *Dilly the Dinosaur* stories, published by Piccadilly Press and Magnet. I've also written two books of poetry, *Smile, Please!* and *All Together Now!*